the
sisters of APF

Also by Zane

Addicted
The Heat Seekers
The Sex Chronicles: Shattering the Myth
Gettin' Buck Wild: Sex Chronicles II
Shame on It All
Nervous
Skyscraper

Edited by Zane

Chocolate Flava: The Eroticanoir.com Anthology

the
sisters of APF

the indoctrination of soror ride dick

zane

ATRIA BOOKS

New York London Toronto Sydney

ATRIA BOOKS
1230 Avenue of the Americas
New York, NY 10020

ISBN: 0-7434-6698-5
       0-7434-7625-5 (Pbk)

First Atria Books trade paperback edition April 2004

10 9 8 7 6 5 4 3 2 1

ATRIA BOOKS is a trademark of Simon & Schuster, Inc.

Manufactured in the United States of America

For information regarding special discounts for bulk purchases, please contact
Simon & Schuster Special Sales at 1-800-456-6798 or business@simonandschuster.com

This novel is dedicated to my loving husband
and best friend, Wayne,
and to the sorors of Alpha Phi Fuckem Sorority, Inc.
www.alphaphifuckem.com
You didn't know?

acknowledgments

With every book, writing acknowledgments becomes harder because I am always afraid that I will leave someone "important" out. The fact is that everyone is important to me. So, if for some reason you do not see your name here, please forgive a tired, pregnant woman for the oversight.

God is still number one on my list and forever will be. Every day is a gift. Every day is a challenge. That is what I live for. Without His blessings, none of us would be here and that is something that should never be regarded as a given.

To my parents, who are celebrating their 50th Wedding Anniversary a couple of months after this book comes out, you are an inspiration to those of us that are just in the early stages of married life. Fifty years is truly a lifetime and I cannot think of a more adoring couple. Thanks for raising me, sustaining me, and being the coolest parents on the earth. It is not easy to accept that your daughter writes "sex books," but your love has only gotten stronger for me and I appreciate it and both of you.

To my husband, Wayne, I do not have to tell you the level of importance you have in my life because I attempt to show that to you every day. In return, I get pampered and showered with love so it is an even trade-off. Like you always say, our relationship is not 50/50 but 100/100.

To my kids, Mommy loves and adores you. I am so proud of all of your accomplishments, and the joy you bring into my life can never be measured. To my son, even though your hormones are raging and you are learning to be independent, never forget that I am your best friend and your greatest supporter. To my daughter, the love notes you give me on a daily basis are inspirational and there is not a shadow of doubt that you will follow in my footsteps and become an author. You already are one. To the son I am carrying inside of me, we can barely wait to meet you and as active as you are already, I am sure you will come out putting foot to ass just like your proud papa. To Erica, I am glad to call you my stepdaughter and I am sure that we will only become closer as time goes by.

To my family members: Miss Bettye, Carlita, Charmaine, Rick, David, Aunt Rose, Aunt Margaret, Aunt Neet, Miss Maurice and Uncle Snook, Uncle George and Miss Mary, Joyce and Ed, and all those I am close to, thanks for the support and love.

To my friends: Pamela Crockett, Esq., Destiny Wood, Lisa Fox, Karen Black, Janet Allen, Sharon Johnson, Dee McConneaughy, Denise Barrow, Tracy Crockett, and all the rest of you chicas, thanks for all the laughs, all the cookouts and parties at the crib, and for practically breaking your neck to get to me when you all think I even cough the wrong way. While I do think you all are a bit overprotective at times, there is never a second when I do not appreciate the love. A special shout out goes to Pamela Crockett, M.D., and Cornelia Williams, two of my oldest and dearest friends that are still representing down in Georgia.

To the special kids in my life: Arianna, Ashley, Jazmin, Adam (my teenage godson), Jerlan (my new godson), Tislem, Indira, Briana, Karlin, Brian, Jr., and Nicholas, thanks for making me remember that children are the most precious gifts.

To all the people that honored my wishes on my wedding day and made donations to the Children's National Medical Center in lieu of gifts, thank you for your generous offerings to help make the lives of children suffering from major illnesses brighter. It meant the world to us and your thoughtfulness was heartwarming.

To my agent, Sara Camilli, as always thanks for keeping my best interest at the forefront of every conversation, for always being concerned about my health and impressing upon me the need to get rest. I often get excited about life in general and it is hard to slow down; even for a few seconds.

To my editor, Malaika Adero, thanks for putting up with a free-spirited, controversial writer such as myself. One never knows what I will be turning in next, but you always accept it with grace. Thank you to the rest of the Simon & Schuster family: Carolyn Reidy, Judith Curr, Louise Burke, Demond Jarrett, Brigitte Smith, Dennis Eulau, and the rest of the crew for your unwavering support and encouragement. A special thanks goes out to my publicist, Staci Shands, for all of her hard work on my behalf.

To the Strebor Books International family that is growing by leaps and bounds, thanks for allowing me to share in your dreams. I am honored to be not only your publisher but your friend. You are the authors of the future and I will not give up until all of you get what you deserve. I hope that my readers will support all of you because I would not publish you unless I knew in my heart that they would enjoy your work. So to my readers, please check out: *Daughter by Spirit* and *Everybody Got Issues* by V. Anthony Rivers, *All That and a Bag of Chips* and *Been There, Done That* by Darrien Lee, *Luvalwayz:The Opposite Sex and Relationships* and *Draw Me With Your Love* by Shonell Bacon and JDaniels, *The Last Dream Before Dawn* by D.V. Bernard, *Feenin* by Nane Quartay, *Sex, Lies & Big Mistakes* by Destin Soul, *Love and Justice* by Rique Johnson, *Nyagra's Falls* by Michelle Valentine, *Turkeystuffer* by Mark Crockett, *My Diet Starts Tomorrow* by Laurel Handfield, *Another Man's Wife* by Shonda Cheekes, *Missed Conceptions* by Michelle DeLeon, *Pandora's Box* by Allison Hobbs, *Money for Good* by Franklin White, *Ballad of a Ghetto Poet* by A.J. White, *Passion Marks* by Lee Hayes, and *Jasminium* by Jonathan Luckett. Also check out *Blackgentlemen.com* by myself, Shonda Cheekes, JD Mason (author of *And on the 8th Day She Rested* and *One Day I Saw a Black King*), and Eileen Johnson as well as *Sistergirls.com* by Rique Johnson, Destin Soul, V. Anthony Rivers, William Fredrick Cooper (author of *Six Days in January*), Earl Sewell (author of *Taken for Granted*), and Michael Pressley (author of *Blackfunk* and *Blackfunk II: No Regrets / No Apologies*). Much love goes out to the Strebor Books International staff: Charmaine, Wayne, Andre, and Pamela, as well as all the freelancers that make our lives easier. For more information, check out www.streborbooks.com.

Thanks to all the other authors that have shown me love, respect and support from day one: Eric Jerome Dickey, Margaret

Johnson-Hodge, Sheila Copeland, Tracy Price-Thompson, Karen E. Quinones Miller, Nancy Flowers, Gwynne Forster, Pat G'Orge-Walker, Collen Dixon, Dwayne Birch (I am still your biggest fan and once these publishing houses stop sleeping on you, you are going to be a force to be reckoned with—*Shattered Souls* should have sold 500,000 copies by now), Marlon Green, Anthony Ri'chard, and so many, many more. If I left your name out, insert it here _____. To those authors that have befriended me and then decided to try to stab me in the back, trust me when I say that it all gets back to me. I am not mad; just disappointed. You can't knock the hustle and if you think talking bad about me will help you sell more books, I wish you well. There is enough room at this table for all of us; wake up and realize it.

Thanks to all the distributors, bookstores, book clubs both on- and offline that support my efforts. Thanks to all the radio personalities and reporters that have taken the time out to interview me; especially asha bandele from *Essence* and David Kirkpatrick from the *New York Times*. Thanks to all the people that spread the word about my books because word-of-mouth advertising is what truly sells them. Thanks to all the thousands of people that email me weekly to tell me to keep my head up and not listen to the "haters." Do not worry; nothing and no one can make me change what is in my heart and when I am writing, it is just me and my imagination. We are both off the chain. For the thousands that have requested *Shame on It All Again,* it is coming along with *Shame on It All Forever.* Harmony, Bryce, Lucky, Fatima, and Colette have a long way to go and I love writing about them.

Hubby, close your eyes and skip over this part. *The Sisters of APF: The Indoctrination of Soror Ride Dick* means a lot to me. It was a joy to write and being a member of the sorority itself is even more of a joy.

If I have forgotten anyone, please do not take it personally. I have another book coming out in three months *(Nervous)*, and another one coming out three months after that *(Skyscraper)*, so I will catch you on the next one.

Now sit back, grab a glass of wine, a beer, or some white lightning if you are from South Dakota like the main character in this book and enjoy the escapades of Mary Ann, Patricia, and Olive.

Peace and blessings,
Zane

In the beginning, there was sex. Boring, passionless sex with women in the missionary position looking at the ceiling, wishing men would hurry up and bust a nut so they can get to sleep. That type of meaningless sex lasted for generations—from the days of the caveman, to the days of the covered wagons, to the days of the bouffant—men thinking they can get their jollies off and not give women pleasure in return.

Then change began to take place; right around the time women obtained the right to vote. Women's sexual inhibitions began to vanish. Sistahs began to realize that if they can work hard every day, bring home the bacon and raise a family, then they deserve a little hellified sex in their lives. No, make that a lot of hellified sex.

They started telling men what they liked and disliked in the bedroom. They started teaching men how to please women. Most importantly, women learned how to please themselves.

Now is the time for the revolution!

The female sexual revolution!

As we embark on the new millennium,

it is time for all the real sexual divas

to stand up and be counted.

Embrace your freakiness.

Come out of the closets.

If your man can't handle it,

trade his ass in for one who can.

Where does it all begin?

Who knows?

I know where the revolution begins. It begins
with the illustrious sorors of ALPHA PHI
FUCKEM SORORITY, INC. Every story has a
beginning, a middle, and an end. This is ours.
—Soror Ride Dick

the
sisters of APF

*alpha phi fuckem**

We are a sorority. You won't find us on any college campus, though. Nor will you see us participating in step shows or collecting canned goods for the needy or having parties at a sorority house. We walk alone. We are as close as any sisterhood can get, and we would lay down our lives for each other. We are professional, well-educated women from all walks of life: bankers, lawyers, accountants, doctors, teachers. We are the proud sorors of Alpha Phi Fuckem Sorority, and we are here to stay.

We were founded over twenty years ago in a penthouse overlooking the Potomac River in Georgetown, an upper-class

---

*Excerpted from *The Sex Chronicles: Shattering the Myth* (Pocket Books, 2002).

area of Washington, D.C. Most of the founding members have moved on, but they're always around to guide us if ever we need their wisdom. A classmate at law school inducted me into the sorority eight years ago. Her name's Patricia, and she's my mentor, having been in the sorority a good two years before myself.

Currently, there are twenty-four active members of the Washington, D.C., chapter. Yes, there are other chapters. There are seven chapters altogether, with sistahs in about three or four other cities trying to form groups now. We have the D.C. chapter and others in New York City, Chicago, Los Angeles, Detroit, Atlanta, and Miami. We even have an annual convention under the ruse of an African-American female business organization. At least, that's what we tell the hotels where we stay.

It takes a significant amount of time to start a chapter because it takes a certain type of woman to be eligible for membership. What are the requirements? First of all, you have to be able to pass an initiation. Every aspect of your life is scrutinized and gone over with a fine-toothed comb. We have to all feel comfortable around you and feel you have that edge about you that sets you apart from other women. We have to feel you are deserving enough to participate in our erotic adventures.

Secondly, you must be trustworthy, secretive, and willing to take all the freaky shit we do to your grave. No one outside the sorority can ever know the things we do. You must be willing to lie to your husband or boyfriend or, in some cases, your girlfriend about where you're going and what you're doing. We all lie, but the sexual gratification we get as our reward is well worth it. We give a whole new outlook to the word *creeping.*

The men we engage in our little escapades are not in the position to tell on us, mostly because they have no idea who the hell we are. We're just faces and bodies, tits and ass, to them. However, the members of the sorority all know who the others are, and therefore, it's important that the trust is there. We could all lose our reputations, possibly even our careers, if the existence of Alpha Phi Fuckem ever came to light.

Thirdly, and this is by far the most important qualification, you have to straight up love fucking. There is just no getting around that, but it goes beyond the normal spectrum of society's definition of fucking. You have to be down for whatever, whenever, and with whomever. No limitations, no inhibitions, and no mental hang-ups are allowed. You must be a woman looking to take sexuality to another level.

Let me give you a quick overview of our mission. We have two "gatherings" a month. The first one is indeed a business meeting. Like I said, we're all professional women. We have an investment club where we pool our resources and invest in certain stocks and bonds. It's each member's responsibility to bring detailed information to the meeting pertaining to at least one corporation and/or product. After all of the options have been discussed, we decide as a group what new investments we will undertake. We also discuss the profits and losses of the stocks already in our portfolio and decide whether to increase or decrease our shares. We have quite a portfolio established. It is a very lucrative investment for all those involved.

The second "gathering" of the month is what we affectionately call Freak Night. Each month, two members are selected at random to organize an activity for the month. The activity chosen must be both sexually stimulating and completely off the hook. Allow me to elaborate. For example, two months ago in January, Yolanda and Keisha decided to host a night of checkers. Yes, I said checkers. Checkers with a twist. Our two sorors rented a ski chalet up in the Shenandoah Mountains of Virginia, a couple hours drive from D.C. It was a huge chalet with six bedrooms, huge whirlpools, a great room, and a breathtaking view of the ski slopes.

It was snowing heavily when we arrived at the top of the mountain. We all met up at the chalet. Patricia and I rode up together in her Mercedes ATV. After all the young ladies had arrived, Yolanda and Keisha went over the agenda for the evening before the men showed up. As usual, the men my sistahs selected were right on point. We all have the same general taste in men, and that's a good thing, because there are never any complaints. Where they found them, who knows? They were somebody's sons, somebody's husbands, somebody's lovers, somebody's babies' daddies. Who cares as long as the sex is good!

The men arrived one, two, and three at a time. Some knew each other already, if they were "picked up" together. All of them were taken off guard when they entered the chalet. In every room throughout the house, there were butt-naked women strategically positioned in front of a checkerboard, including myself. They were informed by the two hostesses, both of whom greeted them naked at the door, that they could challenge the lady of their choice to a game. Imagine their shock to arrive at what they were told would be a cocktail party and discover a virtual smorgasbord of pussy instead.

So play checkers we did, after asking all the men to get naked as well. They were all down because they knew something like that would probably never happen to them again. Maybe in a wet dream, but not during waking hours. We played checkers everywhere—at the dining room and kitchen tables, on the coffee table, on the hearth of the fireplace, on all the beds, on huge stuffed floor pillows. Everywhere. We chatted with the men about the typical things people would talk about at a cocktail party and served them drinks when they requested them so they could see our tits and ass as we walked across the room to get their drinks.

Their dicks were all degrees of hard and came in all different lengths and degrees of thickness. I love dick more than I love my next breath, so they were all mighty appealing to me. I played checkers with a guy from Baltimore. He offered his name. I declined to accept it and refused to give mine. Instead of calling each other by our real names when men are present, we call each other by nicknames like Soror Deep Throat, Soror Cum Hard, and Soror Ride Dick. Yeah, it's silly but we're not trying to impress anyone. It's extremely vital that our real identities remain sacred.

We sat there in the snow-covered chalet for most of the evening playing checkers and shooting the breeze. Wet pussies were everywhere because all of us are multiorgasmic. Just looking at all the dick in the house made us horny as hell. Then came the highlight of the evening, and just in the nick of time too. One more game of checkers without getting some dick, and I was going to start fingering myself and eating my own dayum pussy.

Yolanda and Keisha told everyone it was time to get busy and turned some classic fuck songs on the boom box, the kind of songs that immediately bring fucking to the mind and cease any and all other brain activity. You know the kind. At that point, we all went to fucking. We each fucked the gentleman we had played checkers with the first go-round, and then it turned into a straight up fuckfest. Dicks, tits, ass, pussy everywhere.

Soror Deep Throat, an ophthalmologist during the day, sucked off about every man in there. As usual, I thought she was going for the title in the world records book. My sistah loves sucking some dick more than any woman I have ever known. She comes to the gatherings more to suck dick than to fuck. Soror Cum Hard, a professor of paleontology, is the exact opposite. She loves to be eaten, and by as many men as she can muster up the energy to feed in one night.

Soror Ride Dick would be none other than myself, an assistant district attorney. I avidly believe in the more the merrier. I don't know what it is about riding a dick that turns my ass out, but I love it. Maybe it's having all the control and watching men shiver and lose command of the English language when you're an expert on riding a dick like I am. It takes skills to ride a man in such a fashion that he wants to get in the fetal position and cry afterward because it was so dayum good.

It was a great orgy, as they all are. Everyone left completely sated and with smiles on their faces the next morning. Patricia and I discussed the highlights of the night before as we cautiously descended the icy mountain road, passing a family of deer walking in single file, tracking footprints through the snow.

Anyway, that was the gist of our January activity. February was just as intriguing. Sorors Lisa and Melanie undertook the task of planning a very special Valentine's Day dance. They paid the owner of a sleazy strip club an exorbitant amount of money, in cash of course, to rent the entire place for one evening. They filled the small place up with men in suits, and we each took turns taking the stage and stripping our asses off. All of us wore masks—the kind with feathers you find in abundance at the Mardi Gras. We wore all sorts of sexy lingerie, but ended up in the raw by the end of our individual performances.

Once each lady finished her performance, she would get the opportunity to choose which man she wanted to sit with at a table. At that point, she had to continue her exhibition by sitting facing the man, with one leg thrown up on the table. This enabled him to get an eagle's-eye view of her pussy. He watched while she fucked herself with the ten-inch dildo placed on each table by the hostesses, along with anal beads, butt plugs, and Ben Wa balls to use later on in the evening.

After the last performance, Soror Three Input, a network analyst, pulled a man onstage and showed us a captivating rendition of ass-fucking. It's her personal favorite. Once her interpretation of the fine art of anal sex was over, we had a free-for-all. I made the man I was with get down on his knees underneath the table and eat my pussy while I sucked my own pussy juices off the dildo, and we proceeded from there. He was a great lover, and sometimes I hate the fact that we can never see these men again. It's such a waste when they have the bomb-ass dick.

Just two nights ago, Patricia and I hosted the March gathering. We decided to go back in time and get a little psychedelic thing going. We convinced this guy to let us use his photography studio for the evening. It was in a huge loft, so we had plenty of space. We told all the sorors to wear some bell-bottoms, platforms, crocheted tank tops, halters, or whatever, along with Afro wigs, and meet us there. We found some cool-ass men for the night, including the photographer. That was part of the deal for letting us use his place. Once everyone got there, we turned on the black-light bulbs and strobe lights and danced, getting butt-naked as we went along. Once everyone was nude and doing the hustle, the bump, and the dog to old-school jams, we passed out tubes of neon body paint in various colors and had everyone paint each other. We even had small paint rollers so the men could roll paint onto our asses and wherever else.

Patricia and I had completely covered the hard wood floor with white sheets so we didn't leave a mess. The way everyone was naked and glowing in the dark was wild, especially when the fucking began. We had the photographer take several rolls of film. This was definitely one for the scrapbooks. It was safe because it was so dark in the place that only the body paints and outlines of bodies were visible. Seeing the mass orgy of neon bodies rolling around on the floor was nothing short of amazing.

Well, that brings us up to date. Next month, Sorors Diane and Cynthia are in charge. I can hardly wait to see what they have in store. I realize all of this must seem crazy to outsiders, but trust me, it's not as preposterous as it sounds. The sorority of Alpha Phi Fuckem has already survived for twenty years, and we will survive for a hundred more. One of the founding members is now a governor. She was keynote speaker at our last year's national convention. We're not just some group of women who have fly-by-night ideas, do something for a little while, and get tired of it. We're determined to keep this sorority alive. Just as determined as we are with all the other aspects of our lives.

You would never be able to pick us out as we walk down the street, volunteer at community events, bake cookies for the church bake sales, and act as cheerleaders on the sidelines at our kids' Little League games. Most women have an undercover freak in them yearning to get loose. If we can free our bodies, then we can also free our minds. Soror Ride Dick, over and out!

The events in this novel take place between August 1994 and March 1995.

1

mary ann

"Mary Ann!" My father's voice roared up the stairwell and startled me out of my trance. "You better get a move on or you'll miss the bus!" he said as I was enthralled in the mishaps of a blue jay on my windowsill. The same blue jay that had visited me on a regular basis for the past two years.

"I'm coming, Daddy!" I got up off my bed and threw a stack of journals into my duffel bag. I had already managed to cram most of my meager wardrobe into the trunk my mother gave me—a hand-me-down that once belonged to my great-grandmother. My duffel bag held the most important items though: all of my favorite photographs, my collection of show ribbons I won over the years in junior horseback riding competitions, and my journals.

There was no way I would leave my journals behind for my younger siblings or, God forbid, my parents to find. My life had not been all that exciting up to now—in fact, I wished I had more scandal to write about. Still, the pages contained my private thoughts and my personal history. They were for my eyes only.

"Mary Ann, don't make me have to come up there and get you!" Daddy yelled again. He was obviously more nervous than I was about my leaving home for law school in Washington, D.C. He had been worked up for more than a month, trying to make sure I had everything that I needed for the trip. Granted, moving from South Dakota clear across the country was a major undertaking for me. I had never been outside my home state. I did my undergraduate work at a local college so I could stay close to my parents and help them out with the chicken farm and in the raising of my rambunctious sisters and brothers. I am the eldest of nine. I felt guilty about leaving them all behind but attending Hartsdale Law School had always been a dream of mine. I had worked hard to get accepted, basically giving up my social life to make sure I had good enough grades. I lucked out. I was offered a scholarship so I was flat out of excuses not to leave.

The night before my departure, my twelve-year-old sister Caroline came into my room and pleaded with me not to go. It was one of the hardest conversations of my entire life and ended with both of us in tears. By the time she returned to the bedroom she shared with Liza and Amelia, I think I had managed to convince her that I was doing the right thing. Nonetheless, I was dreading going downstairs to say goodbye. I just knew it would be emotional and depressing.

"Mary Ann!" I could really hear the irritation in my daddy's voice. "Get a move on! Now!"

I grabbed my duffel bag off the bed, looked around my cozy bedroom one last time, and tried to let it all sink in. I took a mental photograph of the teddy bear collection on my window seat, the flowery pink wallpaper, and my thirteen-inch television that had seen much better days and was missing an antenna for more than three years. I knew that my parents would reassign my bedroom to some of my siblings, so it would be drastically different by the time I returned home for a visit. The scenario would not be one where I would come back ten years later with my husband and children and everything would be exactly as I left it. That only happens in movies.

As I made my way down the steep set of stairs, I tried to fight back the tears. I was twenty-two years old and had no business acting childish about the situation. This move was my decision and I had to live with it. I reached the bottom of the steps, expecting to see several sets of pouted lips and soggy eyes. Instead, I had the shock of my life. A chorus of cheers began.

"Mary Ann! Mary Ann! She's our woman! If she can't do it, no one can!" All of my family members had raised their voices for me and I was overwhelmed. They had painted posters and draped colorful streamers all over the living room and dining room area. Each of my siblings took turns giving me cards they had made for me and presents.

By the time I walked out onto the porch ten minutes later, my duffel bag was filled to the brim with everything from a spinning top and black baby doll to a small collection of baseball cards and the sack of country-ham biscuits my mother made me for the bus.

I hugged all of my siblings in the house. Only my mother followed me onto the porch while Daddy went around back to get his pickup truck from the detached garage.

I turned to face my mother but had trouble making eye contact. "I'm going to miss you, Momma," I stated in a barely audible voice. "I'm going to miss everybody so much." Somehow I had managed to stay dry-eyed through the well-wishing inside, but not now.

My mother lifted my chin, forcing me to look into her eyes. "We love you, Mary Ann. Your father and I are extremely proud of you."

"I know that, Momma." I gave her a huge bear hug and whispered in her ear, "I'll continue to make you proud of me. I promise."

She pulled back from me slightly and gathered my head in both of her hands. I noticed the age lines on her face for the very first time. But she was still beautiful with her perfect mocha complexion, deep-set brown eyes, and high cheekbones.

"Mary Ann, I know that you'll do your best at law school and that's all we can ask from you."

"But the kids, Momma," I protested. "How will you and Daddy manage without me?"

She started giggling. "We'll miss you dearly but, trust me, we can handle that group of rowdy chaps in there."

I laughed along with her. "Yeah, but you have to admit they can be a handful."

"No more so than you were." She kissed me lightly on the cheek. "In fact, you were two handfuls."

I glanced at my watch and realized I had less than an hour before the bus left. It would take at least forty minutes for Daddy to make it into town. He drove at a snail's pace.

"I have to go, Momma." I gave her another hug and clenched my eyes shut. The tears were flowing whether I wanted them to or not. "I'll call you as soon as I get settled in the dorm."

"Bye, baby!"

I ran down the porch steps just as my father was pulling around the house. I leapt into the passenger side, slammed the door, and covered my face with my hands. I didn't want my mother to see more crying.

Daddy pulled off with a jerk and didn't say a word to me until we got on the highway a good fifteen minutes later. I had managed to calm down some, but my breathing was still shallow. He placed his hand on my knee. "Mary Ann, it's going to be okay." As I looked over at him, he had a cinematic smile on his face. "I hear Washington, D.C., is a great city to live in. Full of opportunities for lawyers."

"I'm not a lawyer yet, Daddy," I managed to utter. "I haven't even officially started law school yet."

"True, but in three years you'll be a lawyer. A damn good one at that."

I grinned at him. He always managed to brighten the darkest of days. "I'm glad you have so much confidence in me."

"Hell, you're a Ferguson and what a Ferguson wants, a Ferguson gets!"

"Daddy, if that were true, then I would be able to stay in South Dakota and attend Hartsdale Law."

"Well, a Ferguson gets *almost* anything they want." He chuckled. Both of our moods turned solemn and we fell silent once again for a few seconds. "Hey, have you heard the one about the bald chicken and the blue pig?"

"Oh boy, not another joke!" I wasn't really in the right frame of mind for his silly chicken jokes but I humored him. "Go ahead and tell it, Daddy!"

He had me laughing all the way to the bus depot, babbling on and on about chickens. Beyond his family, chickens are my father's entire life. In fact, chicken farming has been the occupation of my family for generations. My great-grandparents lived in the same farmhouse where I grew up. I was going to miss home something terrible: the ten-foot-high ceilings, the fireplace in the dining room, the view of the sunset from the loft of the barn.

We arrived at the bus station ten minutes before bus 1013 was due to depart. My daddy rushed to get my trunk off the bed of the truck and underneath the bus before they slammed the cargo section shut. Afterward, we stood on pins and needles, neither one of us wanting to say goodbye.

"I don't have to go, Daddy," I blurted out.

"Yes you do," he quickly replied. "This is what you've always wanted. You've worked hard for this and, gosh darnit, you're going to go as far as that brain of yours will take you."

"What if I'm not good enough for them?"

"You're good enough for everybody. You're just not *for* everybody. Don't let anyone tell you any different." He threw his arm around my shoulder and pulled me close. "Now get on that bus and call us when you get to D.C."

I grasped onto his waist for dear life. "Thanks for bringing me into this world, Daddy. Thanks for everything."

"No, thank you." He brushed his lips across my forehead and then pushed me away from him toward the steps of the bus. "Get on now."

I was halfway up the steps when I turned to look at him one more time, all six feet five inches of him. I toppled back down the steps, threw my arms around his neck, and gave him a big wet one on his left cheek. "Bye, Daddy!"

"Bye, sweetheart!"

I got settled on the bus and waved at him as he got back in his truck and abruptly pulled off. I guess watching the bus depart would have been too much for him. My daddy hates to show emotion. He thinks it is a sign of male weakness. I think showing how you feel is a sign of sincerity, but he is one of those old-fashioned men who could never comprehend such a notion.

No sooner had the bus pulled away than I spotted Clarence running around the corner by the feed store flailing his arms and screaming my name. "Mary Ann! Mary Ann!"

I placed my palm up against the cool glass of the window and then waved at him. He looked frustrated, depressed, and disappointed. I guess he thought he might have changed my mind the last time we were together.

Clarence was my high school sweetheart and the only lover I had ever had. While I didn't think he was an exceptional lover,

I didn't have anyone to compare to him. I probably wasn't exceptional myself. After all, I was very timid when it came to sex. Good girls don't engage in lewd sexual acts. That's how I was raised. That was the bottom line.

Clarence and I had gathered up enough nerve to watch some porno films on a couple of occasions. They seemed to make him uncomfortable. But I, on the other hand, was enthralled by sexy movies. I couldn't believe women actually performed certain sex acts without passing out or gagging on the huge dicks of the men in those flicks.

Saying goodbye to Clarence was difficult. I wished I could have taken him with me to D.C. but it just wasn't fathomable. He was in training to take over his father's carpentry business and there was no way he could leave town. We were together for the last time three nights before. We spent time together in the small, cramped apartment he rented above the local convenience store on Main Street. He begged me to stay and I begged him to stop begging me for something I couldn't give him. We fell asleep drenched in each other's tears and sweat from making love.

Seeing him standing there on the corner—finer than frog's hair with his curly black hair, bronze complexion, and sparkling hazel eyes—made me want to tell the bus driver as we pulled away to stop and let me off. I couldn't though. I had to do what I had to do. In time, I would get over Clarence. I didn't have a choice.

I settled back into my seat and spoke to the elderly white woman who had claimed the aisle seat beside me. She seemed friendly enough. She was headed to Alexandria, Virginia, to see her four grandchildren. She almost talked my ear off, bragging about them and flashing their wallet-sized photos at me. I fell asleep a few hours later, even though it was only mid-morning. I had a long trip and an even longer law school experience ahead of me. I hoped I could handle it.

2

patricia

Another year of law school. Damn, would it ever end! I didn't know what compelled me to throw my name in the campus lottery for resident assistant in Myers Hall. I figured the extra spending money, even though it was a small stipend, was better than nothing at all. I was doing well with the investments I made through the sorority, but every little bit helps when you're a struggling student.

As I stood there in the hallway, watching the women who would be placed under my charge, most of them were exactly what I expected: beauty queens, all trying to outdo each other with clothing and makeup. I couldn't imagine how the school administrators expected me to regulate the comings and goings of grown women. They were adults. Surely everyone was getting sexed in some form or fashion and they didn't need me to school them on morality. That's for damn sure! Not the way I like to get my freak on.

I was just about to go into my room and start unpacking my CD collection when I spotted her. She was dragging a trunk up the sixth-floor steps that must have outweighed her two to one. It wasn't so much that she looked innocent to me. She just looked lost. Not lost in the literal sense but lost *period*.

It was hot as hell in D.C. and yet she was dressed like she was on her way to the Poconos for a weekend of skiing. She had on a long-sleeved wool sweater, a plaid shirt, a pair of black leggings that looked more like long johns, heavy wool socks, and tattered brown leather ankle boots.

I walked down to the end of the hall to the stairwell and grabbed one of the handles on the trunk, trying to prevent it from dragging her all the way back down the steps.

She glanced up at me with huge brown eyes and flashed a perfect set of teeth. "Thank you!"

"Not a problem." I helped her get the trunk up the remaining three steps and then we let it fall to the ground with a thud. I reached out my hand. "I'm Patricia Reynolds, the resident assistant."

As she shook my hand I noticed she was trembling from head to foot. I thought her teeth were going to chatter. "Mary Ann. Mary Ann Ferguson."

"Are you cold or something? You're shaking like a leaf." It was a silly question, but I asked it anyway.

"No, I'm fine really," she replied hesitantly. "I'm just a little nervous about all of this."

"Where are you from?" I couldn't quite place her accent.

"South Dakota."

"South Dakota!" I exclaimed.

She looked like she was about to pass out in embarrassment. "Yes, is there something wrong with South Dakota?"

"No, I just didn't realize there were any black people in South Dakota."

She giggled, the first sign of easing off her obvious panic attack. "There aren't many there. That's for sure."

"Well, I assume you've noticed that there are plenty of them in D.C."

"Indeed. Now I see why they call it the Chocolate City."

"Lots of fine men here too, gurl," I assured her, just in case she was wondering. "I don't care what anyone says. D.C. has the finest collection of brothas I've ever seen, and being that I'm originally from New York, that's saying something."

"New York City!" She looked like she was in shock. "I've never met anyone from New York City before!"

I fell out laughing. "You're going to meet plenty of them around here."

Mary Ann lowered her eyes to the floor. "I've never been out of South Dakota before," she admitted, seemingly full of shame.

"How did you get here? Plane?"

"Naw, I caught the bus. I couldn't afford a plane. I'm here on a scholarship," Mary Ann said, as if it was something dreadful.

"Hell, so am I."

"Really?" Mary Ann smiled.

"Word up! So Mary Ann, what room are you in?"

"I think I'm in 618 but I'm not quite sure. Let me check." She rummaged through this large duffel bag on her shoulder and retrieved a crumpled piece of paper. I had to refrain from cackling when I saw the baby doll in her bag. I thought, this chick seriously has issues. She unfolded the paper. "Yes, 618."

"Cool. That's directly across the hall from my room. I'm in 617."

"Oh, okay," she whispered.

"Come on, it's right down here on the left." I grabbed one of the handles on the trunk and waited for her to get the other one.

She shoved the paper back in her bag and helped me drag the trunk seventy or so feet to her room. We got it inside and threw it on the bare mattress.

"This is a nice room," she announced. I didn't see anything glamorous about the dorm rooms, but I nodded my head in agreement just the same. "I get the room all to myself? I figured I would have a roommate."

"Not in this dorm. Law school dormitories are single rooms and coed. A roommate might hinder studying. At least, that's what the bigwigs say."

"Did you just say *coed?*"

"Yes, coed as in both men and women," I responded with a raised brow. "We're all grown here. This is an all-female floor but every other floor is male."

"Oh." She seemed to relax slightly. "What about the bathrooms and showers? Are they coed?"

"Nope." I closed her bedroom door so I could point to the

bathroom door in the corner that was hidden behind it. "Everyone has their own bathroom. Can you imagine the freaky shit that would be going on up in here if the showers were coed?" I fell out laughing. She sank down on the bed beside her trunk. I couldn't help being nosy. It's my nature. "Mary Ann, are you scared of men or something?"

"No, of course not," she replied with an edge of sarcasm in her voice. "That's ridiculous. I'm twenty-two."

I threw my palms up in her direction. "Hey, I was just asking. You seem kind of edgy every time I mention the male species."

"I had a boyfriend, Clarence, back in South Dakota," she boasted. I guess she wanted me to know that she was capable of getting a man, despite her homely appearance.

"Had? Did you two break up recently?"

"Very recently," she uttered getting up and walking toward the window overlooking the courtyard. "We broke up the other day."

"How come?" Okay, I'm *extremely* nosy. Shoot me already.

"I didn't see any reason to have him wait on me for three years." She swung around and faced me. "He's a man, you know, and he has certain needs."

"Shoot, women have needs too."

"Yeah, but not like men."

That's when I knew it. That's when I knew she was sexually repressed and oppressed like the majority of my female counterparts. That's when I knew she probably just laid there and let men have their way with her, not even worrying or expecting an orgasm for herself.

"Whatever you say, gurlfriend." I opened her door back up and stepped out into the hall. "Listen, I'm about to make my rounds and introduce myself to the rest of the women on the floor. Particularly the sistahs. We have to stick together on campus. United we stand, divided we fall."

"It was nice meeting you, Patricia, and thanks for the help with my trunk."

"Don't mention it." I was about to walk away but hesitated. The chick was going to have major problems fitting in. That was *too* obvious. "Mary Ann, I'm going to walk over to the cafeteria a little later for dinner. You want to walk with me?"

"Sure! That would be great!" That was the most excitement she had shown in the fifteen minutes since I laid eyes on her. "What time are you going over?"

"Say about six. Is that cool with you?"

"Six would be fine, thank you."

"Um, Mary Ann."

"Yes?"

"If you and I are going to be hanging, then . . ."

"Hanging?"

"Yes, going out together. *Hanging.*" She was really out of it. "Attending different social functions together."

"Oh." She finally got it and it was about damn time. "Hanging."

I continued. "If you and I are going to be hanging, you'll have to loosen up a bit."

"What do you mean by that?" She was obviously offended. She held out the bottom of her sweater. "Is there something wrong with my clothing?"

"Actually, I was referring to your tense demeanor. However, now that you mentioned your clothing, you look like you're headed to Alaska." She rolled her eyes at me. Good, at least she did have some fire in her. "You want to borrow something more appropriate for this weather from me?"

"No, I have something to wear," she declared.

"Okay, cool. I'll see you at six." I left it at that and walked off. I had barely made it ten feet when I heard her door slam like a clap of thunder.

mary ann

Okay, so I wasn't a fashion model. She didn't have to come off at me like that. Just because I was a little nervous about my new surroundings didn't mean I was a church mouse. As for my clothes, it had been freezing on the bus and I've always been cold-natured. I unlatched the rusty trunk locks and started unpacking my things into the three-drawer dresser on the opposite wall from the bed.

I didn't own a lot of name-brand clothes and no designer clothes. I never saw the reasoning behind advertising someone else's name on my body and paying out the behind for the privilege to do it. That's ludicrous! I picked out a pair of khakis and a white poplin blouse to wear to dinner and then hit the shower.

The warm water felt great and the high water pressure was an added bonus. The water pressure back on the farm was always limited. I used some of the bath gel Clarence bought me as a going-away present. It must've set him back a pretty penny. It was the aromatherapy kind they sell in fancy department stores. It was relaxing, just like the bottle claimed it to be.

Afterward, I made my bed with the new set of crisp white sheets and the pink wool blanket my mother gave me. The mattress left a lot to be desired. It had a couple of springs protruding through the cover and I had to toss and turn a little bit to get comfortable. I made a mental note to ask Patricia about the possibility of getting a new one at dinner.

Long bus trip or not, I was too busy worrying about how I would fit in at Hartsdale to take a nap. Namely, Patricia seemed nice enough, although her parting comments pissed me off. She was lucky I didn't slam the door in her face. Rather, I waited until she was down the hall a ways and slammed it. One thing was obvious: I had always been one to bite my tongue in certain situations but all of that was going to have to change in the big city.

I had actually begun to doze off when Patricia started banging on my door. Luckily, I had dressed fully before I laid down. I flung the door open and was stunned. Patricia had on a hoochie momma dress, a complete contrast to the shorts and loose tee she was wearing when I met her. The dress was short, red, and tight enough to see her heart pounding in her partially exposed chest.

She had pinned her long wavy black hair up, leaving only a few strands dangling on the left side of her perfectly sculptured sienna face. She glared at me with her dark gray eyes while I let her outfit sink in. "Is there something wrong?"

"Uh-uh-uh, naw," I finally managed to utter. "I was just admiring your outfit," I lied.

She giggled at me. "Yeah, right!"

"I'm serious. It's very becoming." I was stretching the truth but it really was becoming on her. She had the body for it and, more importantly, the nerve to actually wear it. "I really like the dress."

"Cool, I have a black one just like it. You want me to go get it so we can be twins at dinner?"

She called my bluff big time. "No, thanks," I quickly replied. "I'm fine with what I have on."

She smirked at me, inhaling my bullshit, and then grabbed the doorknob. "So you ready?"

"Ready." I wasn't ready, but I couldn't hole up in my dorm room forever. After all, this was what I had always dreamed of. "Is the cafeteria a long way?"

"Naw, just through the courtyard. It's a short walk."

"Okay." I was debating about changing my shoes. I had on some burgundy penny loafers that weren't too comfortable. I decided to chance it since she said it wasn't far. "I'm ready."

We got out in the hallway and I headed toward the steps. "Um, Mary Ann," Patricia called after me. I turned and she was headed in the opposite direction. "Why don't we just take the elevator?"

"Elevator?" I asked, turning red with embarrassment. "You mean there's an elevator?"

"Yes, we're living in modern times around here."

"I didn't see an elevator when I came in."

"That's because you came in the back entrance."

I couldn't help but laugh. "You mean to tell me I lugged that trunk up six flights of stairs for nothing?"

Patricia fell out laughing. "You damn sure did!"

. . .

Patricia and I laughed the entire time to the cafeteria. While it wasn't quite as short a walk as she proclaimed it to be, my feet managed to hold up well.

It was a madhouse when Patricia and I entered the dining hall on the bottom level of the student union. The returning students were hugging all over each other and slapping their buddies on the back, ecstatic to see their classmates after the long summer.

It was easy to pick out the first-year law students. They all looked nervous and out of place, just like me. Being there with Patricia made me a little less nervous and I didn't even feel ashamed when I pulled out my free-meal card because she whipped hers out too.

She introduced me to some of her friends while we stood in line. They all seemed nice enough. Once we sat down, the strangest thing happened. This expensively clad sistah walked up to our table to speak to Patricia.

"Hey soror, what's up?" she asked, placing a finely mani-cured hand on Patricia's shoulder. Patricia leered at her and stared her down, refusing to blink. "I mean, I mean, I meant . . ." the woman stuttered. This is strange, I thought.

"Yvette, this is Mary Ann. Mary Ann, this is Yvette." Patricia turned back to her plate and picked up a spoonful of processed mashed potatoes.

Yvette mumbled a quick greeting to me before quickly walking away.

I glanced at Patricia, who was staring out one of the picture windows. She appeared to be extremely upset. I had never joined a sorority—black ones were scarce in South Dakota—but I was under the impression that sorors treated one another with love and respect, not disdain.

"So what sorority are you in?" I ventured to ask.

Patricia gasped, darting her eyes at me like I had just broken her out of a trance. "Huh? What did you say?"

"What sorority do you belong to? AKA, Delta, Sigma Gamma Rho?"

"Uh no, none of those," Patricia answered hesitantly.

"Then which one?"

"I'm not in one." Patricia chuckled. "Yvette's just plain ole silly. She and I go way back. We went to high school together in New York."

"Oh." That made absolutely no sense to me so I dropped the subject.

"Back in the day," Patricia decided to elaborate on her explanation, "we were in this club called the Vogue Club. You know, the most popular, best-dressed girls in the school, and we used to refer to each other as sorors from time to time. That's all."

"I see." While that made it a little clearer, the evil look she threw her soror still made me wonder if I was yet privy to the entire story. "Patricia, can I ask you something?"

"Sure."

"Why are you being so friendly to me?"

"Why wouldn't I be? You're new here, you're rooming right across the hall, and besides, I hate to eat alone."

I took a sip of my Coke, which was seriously flat, through a straw. "Well, I appreciate it. You're the first person I've really met except for the people over at the housing department and they were pretty nasty."

Patricia giggled. "Let me tell you something about people around here. In particular, the administration. They all feel like they are doing us a favor. Especially those of us here on scholarship. They don't realize how hard we have worked to get here, but in the long run, once we graduate from law school and start pulling down those phat checks, they'll be making chicken change compared to you and me."

"From your lips to God's ears." I took a bite of my cheeseburger. It tasted like rubber. Some things don't change from campus to campus. The food was horrible. My friends from college used to help me boil hot dogs about an hour or two after they stopped serving dinner in the cafeteria and we would sell them door-to-door for a dollar each. People would snatch them up, even though we didn't have condiment the first. "I need to make a lot of money so I can help my family out back home."

"You come from a large family?"

"Yes, I have eight brothers and sisters."

"Damn, that's deep," Patricia said, looking stunned. "I'm an only child and that's a good and bad thing. Good because I never had to share and bad because I was often lonely."

"I can't imagine not having my siblings in my life. It would be so, so empty."

We sat there in silence for a couple of minutes gnawing at our nasty food. There was a commotion near the doorway and I turned to see what the ruckus was all about. A tall, handsome brotha had made some sort of grand entrance with a bunch of women running up to him and throwing their arms around his waist and neck.

"Who is that?"

"Girl, don't even ask," Patricia replied, smacking her lips with disdain. "He's nothing but trouble."

"Oh, I see." I continued to stare at him. He had the smoothest skin I had ever seen on a man. He was very dark, a big turn-on for me because I didn't see many men like him when I was growing up. Only in magazines and in the movies. "He's very handsome."

"That he is, but he's also a playa." Patricia sighed heavily before adding, "His name is Trevor Ames and he has made a career of getting the panties."

I almost choked on a french fry. "Getting the panties?"

"Yeah, you know? Don't play dumb."

"Oh, okay, I get your meaning. He tries to get all the women in bed, huh?"

"Yes, and no one ever denies him."

I raised an eyebrow in curiosity, recognizing the bitterness in Patricia's voice. "Did you deny him?"

"Subject dropped," she announced. "Are you done eating?"

"To be honest, I'm afraid if I finish this, I'll be sick for the rest of the night."

"Cool, then let's head on out." Patricia jumped up from the table and grabbed her tray. I followed suit, and after we put the dishes on the kitchen conveyor belt, we walked on back to our dorm. She told me she had to finish unpacking, so I lied and said I needed to do the same. I could tell she was in a rotten mood and I had the distinct feeling Trevor Ames was the underlying cause of it all. I didn't press it though. I just told her good night, went in my room, and pulled out my journal so I could write all about the first day of my new adventure. Afterward, I found the pay phone down the hall, called my parents collect to let them know I had arrived safely, and then hit the sack. Before I could even finish saying my prayers, I was fast asleep.

3

mary ann

I debated for hours over whether or not to attend the mixer in the student union. Then I decided, what the hell? I walked across the hall and knocked on Patricia's door to see if she wanted to *hang*. She wasn't in. I figured she must've been on a hot date with one of those fine-ass men she talked about.

I went back into my room and searched through the measly belongings in my closet. I threw on a black short-sleeved cotton tee and a pair of blue jeans. I had heard that the mixers were informal. People sat around talking about law school while sipping tea and eating pastries. Not my sort of thing, but I was bored. Plus, it was time for me to be sociable with someone other than Patricia.

I walked across the courtyard to the student union and took the stairs up to the rooftop lounge where the mixer was taking place. It was cool outside that evening. I regretted not bringing along a thin sweater, but walking all the way back to get one was out of the question. I just wanted to see what I could see in thirty minutes or less and go.

Most of the people were extremely friendly, to my surprise. I was braced to be confronted by a bunch of prissy stuck-up people. But the more I heard, the more normal they sounded. I felt underdressed though. The women were wearing dresses and the men were in jackets and ties.

I was about to leave and go find something else to put on, when a brotha jumped in my path and flashed a grin at me.

"Hi, I'm Trevor Ames!" he proclaimed, like he was Denzel Washington or some damn body famous.

"I'm Mary Ann," I replied, looking him up and down. I recognized him from the cafeteria. He was the one Patricia was talking big trash about, which meant he was nothing but trouble.

"You have a last name, Mary Ann?" he asked, offering me his hand.

I reluctantly shook it. "Yes, it's Ferguson."

He squinted his eyes and chuckled. "Where are you from?"

I just hated it when people picked up my accent. "South Dakota."

"Wow!" he exclaimed so loudly that I had to take a step back. "D.C. must be quite a culture shock for you."

"I haven't really seen that much of it, but I guess you could say that," I said, shrugging my shoulders. I had to admit that the man was fine. Now that he was standing right beside me, I realized he was much taller than I originally guesstimated. He had to be a good six feet six and was one of the most handsome men on campus. No wonder he was able to do so many hit-and-runs on the women at Hartsdale.

I tried to walk around him but he wasn't havin' it. He propped his elbow on the wall and stopped me dead in my tracks. "What have you seen?"

"The bus station and campus." I giggled, knowing how ridiculous that must've sounded.

"Well, we'll just have to do something about that. D.C. has a lot to offer."

"Yes, I know." I took a deep sigh. He was going to force me to have a conversation, whether I wanted to or not. I decided to keep it simple and then say my farewells. "That's one of the reasons I decided to come here for law school. We used to read all about Washington, D.C., in school and, of course, the movers and shakers on Capitol Hill are always in the news."

Before he could barrel off another question at me, a blond-haired, blue-eyed Barbie doll came prancing up, rudely interrupting us. "Hey, Trevor."

"Hey, FeFe," Trevor replied, looking irritated. He pointed at me. "This is Mary Ann Ferguson. She's in her first year."

"Of course she is," FeFe responded, shaking my hand. Her hands were ice-cold. She needed a sweater a hell of a lot more than I did. "I would have seen her around here before. Nice to meet you, Mary Ann."

We stood there for a few seconds sizing each other up. She was pretty but the name had to go. I thought Mary Ann was a silly name but FeFe sounded like a poodle.

Once she discerned that Trevor and I weren't about to continue our conversation with her standing there, she decided to mark her territory before moving on. "Don't forget you promised to take me to that new club, Sensation," she said, grabbing his elbow off the wall and wrapping her arm around his.

He quickly pulled his arm away. "I didn't forget."

She sized me up one more time and then walked away. "Call me, baby."

I took the opportunity to make an exit. I heard him reply to her, "I'll do that." I was halfway out of the door. "Mary Ann, hold up," I heard him say after me. "Where are you going?"

He covered the space between us swiftly with his long legs and was beside me before I could make a clean getaway. "I'm a bit tired. I think I'll just head back to the dorm."

I glanced around the roof lounge and noticed a group of women staring at us and whispering. He's probably slept with all of them, I thought. I was reminded of Patricia's warning to stay away from him.

"May I walk you?"

I shrugged, swinging open the door and starting down the first flight of steps. "It's up to you. I wouldn't want to take you away from all your female admirers."

"They don't admire me," he said, following behind me. "I'm in my third year and at the top of the class, so I do quite a bit of mentoring."

"I bet," I stated sarcastically. "Does that include shaking your booty at a nightclub? Sensation, wasn't it?"

He grabbed me by the elbow when we reached the bottom-level lobby. "You're jealous," he boasted, obviously basking in the thought. "That's so cute."

"Jealous?" I asked incredulously. "I don't even know you. Just your reputation."

I walked out into the courtyard, hoping he would take a hint, act like an egg and beat it. No such luck.

"Aw, I get it now."

"You get what?" I asked, stopping so I could look up at him. I wanted to see where his head was.

"I saw you eating dinner the other night in the cafeteria with Patricia."

"What of it?"

"She filled your head with a bunch of negative bullshit about me, didn't she?" he asked.

"No need to get hostile." I started to walk again.

"I'm not hostile," he insisted. "I'm just sick of getting the dog-pound treatment from most of the sistahs at school."

"Is that why you date women like FeFe?" I asked, not knowing what kind of woman FeFe really was except for her desperate attempt to make it known at the mixer that she was banging him.

Trevor was the one to stop in his tracks that time. "Damn, don't tell me you're one of those!"

I didn't like or appreciate his tone. "One of what?"

He started walking again since I apparently wasn't stopping. I was cold, tired, and growing increasingly irritated with him. "One of those sistahs that automatically stereotype a brotha as a sellout simply because he can appreciate the beauty of all women."

That did it! "Don't come off on me like that!" I blared, stopping so suddenly that he ran into my heel. I turned around and glared up at him. "I was joking, but obviously you must feel uncomfortable dating outside your race if you jump on the defensive so easily!"

"Whatever!" he stated with disdain.

"Whatever nothing," I persisted. "First off, I'm from South Dakota. Remember? Most of my best friends growing up were white and the first boy I ever made out with in sixth grade was white so don't imply that I'm a racist, because you don't know jack shit about me!"

"Okay, okay!" He raised his palms toward me in defeat.

To this day, I'm not even sure where my words came from but I was going through some sort of transformation. I had always heard that people in the city were insensitive, unfriendly, and mean. I was living up to all those qualities after just three days.

I started walking again. My dorm was in clear view and I was anxious to get there.

"I get your point, Mary Ann, and I apologize."

"Apology accepted," I uttered, trying to calm down because it felt like my heart was skipping every other beat.

"It just pisses me off when I'm out with a white woman, even if she's only a friend, and people stare at us and make disparaging comments."

The conversation was growing tired and I didn't want to *hang* anymore that night. I stopped in front of the dorm. "Well, here's my building. Thanks for walking with me."

"May I see you up to your room?" I couldn't believe my ears. After the conversation we'd just had, he still couldn't take a hint.

"No, thanks," I said, in lieu of the reply that was on the edge of my lips. There was no reason to be nasty because he would have played that jealousy card again, I thought, even though nothing could be further from the truth. Clarence was weighing heavily on my mind and I wasn't interested in sharing a man with FeFe or anyone else for that matter.

"But the night's still young," Trevor protested, pouting. "You don't even know anything about me yet." I know enough and I don't even think so, I said to myself. "You haven't even asked where I'm from."

I took a deep sigh. "Where are you from, Trevor?"

"Gary, Indiana."

"Okay, so now I've asked." I giggled. "Good night."

I walked up the steps to the front door of the dorm.

"Wait, Mary Ann! I was wondering if you'd like to go out sometime? This Friday perhaps?"

I felt bad about shooting the brotha's hopes down but I just couldn't envision dating him, not even once. I was dying to see more of the city but I planned to ask Patricia to show me around.

I tried to think of a tactful response. "I'm still trying to get settled in and everything. Maybe some other time." I had the door open and should have left it at that but my sarcastic twin reared her ugly head. "Besides, your social calendar seems pretty full already."

"What can I say?" Trevor blushed and my heart skipped another beat. Not out of anger but out of a flicker of lust. The moonlight hitting up against his well-defined features made me a bit hot under the collar. "My cup runneth over."

His ego turned me off as quickly as his appearance had turned me on. "Once again, good night, Trevor."

He took the steps two at a time and grabbed the glass door before it could shut completely behind me. "Look, it's obvious you're not down with playing games and neither am I so I'll cut straight to the point."

"What is your point?" I crossed the lobby and pressed the call button on the elevator. "I'm totally exhausted and I'd like to go to bed now."

"I'd like to go to bed with you." I rolled my eyes at him and glared at him with disdain. "Sorry, I couldn't help it." He chuckled. "It's just that I really, *really* like you, Mary Ann."

"Imagine that!" I giggled. "You've only known me for twenty minutes and you're already smitten with me."

I could hear the elevator cranking somewhere behind the closed steel doors and I willed it to hurry the hell up. I was still embarrassed about showing up at the dorm my first day and lugging my trunk up the steps when there was an elevator.

Trevor would just not give up. "Ever since I saw you the other day, I've been thinking of no one but you. You have this classic yet subtle beauty about you."

That's when I knew he was full of shit! I had been described a lot of ways in my lifetime but "classic" and "subtle beauty" were never up in the mix. "In other words, you're looking to add another notch to your belt and you thought you could do a hit-and-run on me before I found out you're a playa? Well, sorry, too late."

"I'm offended!" Trevor whined as the elevator doors slid open.

I stepped on and pushed the button for the sixth floor. He hopped right on behind me. "That makes two of us." I decided to use the opportunity to clarify a few things about myself. He really took me to be a fool. "Just because I'm from the country doesn't mean I was absent the day God handed out common sense." He guffawed at my statement but I was as serious as a heart attack. "I mean, I am here at this prestigious institution. As a matter of fact, I ranked number one in the candidate roster for first-year law students—which is why I have a full scholarship," I boasted, totally surprising myself because I was ashamed of being there on scholarship up until that very second.

He finally stopped laughing and tried to earn a brownie point when the elevator stopped and we got off. "I could tell you were a bookworm. That's one of the things that attracted me to you."

I rummaged through my small handbag to get out my key as I walked down the hall to my room. "Yes, I am a bookworm and I don't have time for the likes of you. Why don't you go back to the mixer and find FeFe or some other member of your harem?" I unlocked my door and stepped inside. He opened his mouth to say something but I preempted him. "I'm going to bed now, whether you like it or not!"

I slammed the door in his face and fell asleep that night proud of myself for evading the dog bite.

4

---

patricia

I woke up around 1 P.M. on Sunday afternoon, physically spent but elated about the night before. Freak nights always worked wonders for my attitude, not to mention my complexion. I flipped through the local network channels on my nineteen-inch TV. All that was on was a bunch of political panel shows, evangelists, and old martial arts movies. That's the one thing I hated about living in dorms. No cable TV.

I took a relaxing bubble bath and threw on some black leggings and an ivory tee. I really needed to study, but didn't feel like it. We were barely two weeks into the semester and the professors were trippin' hard already. I thought the first two years of law school were hard but the third year was shaping up to be pure hell.

I decided to go see what Mary Ann was up to. She kept pretty much to herself and that disturbed me, although I'm not quite sure why. It wasn't like we were bosom buddies or anything. She seemed like cool peoples, just shy.

I tapped on her door and got no response, so I knocked a little harder. I was about to give up and head on back to my room to study tariffs when I saw her getting off the elevator at the far end of the hall. She was dressed in a homely peach dress with a huge white lace collar and a pair of black patent-leather flats. The sistah definitely had some fashion issues to resolve, but after the way she almost threw a hissy fit the first time I critiqued her wardrobe, I wasn't about to make the same mistake twice. At least, not until I got to know her better.

"Hey, Mary Ann. Where are you coming from?" I asked when she had closed about half the distance between us. "I was just looking for you."

She threw her right hand up to her chest like she was about to have a stroke. "Looking for me? How come? I was over at the chapel for the service."

"Just wanted to see if we could hang out today."

"Hang out where?" she asked nervously, unlocking her room once she got to it. I followed her inside. "You mean off campus?"

"Yes, I mean off campus. There's not a damn thing to do around—" I stopped dead in my tracks. "What's all this?" I inquired, referring to the half-dozen or so vases scattered around her room filled with every shade of rose you could imagine.

She giggled, throwing her purse down on her bed. "They're from Trevor. He's been sending them every day for a week."

I was speechless. The Trevor I knew and hated would never venture to give a woman roses. "Surely you don't mean Trevor Ames?"

"Yes, the one you told me about in the dining hall that day."

I sat down on her bed, stunned beyond disbelief. "Let me get this straight. Trevor Ames has been sending you flowers *every* day?"

"Flowers and little notes telling me how much he likes me and wants to get to know me better," she boasted, blushing and grinning from ear to ear. The frown on my face must have been a clue because she added, "I'm sorry if it makes you uncomfortable, Patricia. I won't accept any more of the flowers if it makes you upset."

"*Upset?*" I faked a laugh. "Why would it upset me? If I wanted Trevor, I could have had him a long time ago. He's not my type."

Mary Ann let out a sigh of relief. "Good. You're the only person that has been truly nice to me and I wouldn't want to hurt you in any way. Besides, I don't think Trevor is my type either. Our first encounter didn't go too well."

"How did you meet Trevor?"

"At the mixer last weekend." She kicked off her shoes and slipped into a pair of hot-pink furry slippers. "He walked me back to the dorm and the conversation turned ugly."

"How so?" I asked, being my typically nosy self. "What did you two discuss?"

"Basically, we talked about his dating habits and my morality. I made it perfectly clear that I wasn't interested in some one-night stand or fly-by-night fantasy."

"And?"

"And that was it. I told him I was tired and going to bed."

"So you two didn't kiss or anything?"

She looked at me like I had asked her if she sucked his dick. "Absolutely not! I'm not that type. I just got out of a relationship with Clarence a few weeks ago and it would be totally inappropriate for me to fall into the arms of another man so quickly."

I wanted to puke. Her morality, as she put it, was sickening. I had a feeling that if she ran up on a piece of hellified dick action, all of that would change. She definitely wasn't going to find that with Trevor, so I decided to try to save her the disappointment.

"I sincerely hope you aren't considering dating Trevor because he will use you and dump you just like the rest of the heartbroken women around here."

Mary Ann chuckled. "I will take that under advisement." She sat down on the bed beside me. "So what type of hangin' did you have in mind?" she asked.

I shrugged my shoulders. "Maybe a movie or lunch. Whatever."

She chewed on her bottom lip like she was in serious thought. "Well, if I can do it for ten bucks or less, I'm all for it. I'm on a budget."

"You can't do much in D.C. with ten dollars."

"Well, I guess I will just have to pass, then."

"No, no way, sistahgurl. You've been lurking around this campus enough. Have you even been off campus since you got here?"

"Not really. Just down to the corner store to get some snacks for late-night study sessions."

"Time for a change. Throw on some jeans or something and let's roll out. I'm driving."

Mary Ann grinned. "Okay. Give me a couple of minutes to change."

We rode over to Prince George's Plaza in my hoopty, a silver 1978 Nissan Stanza. Mary Ann almost fell out, seeing all the black people at the mall. "You know, you can walk through the entire mall near my old college and be hard-pressed to see one other black person."

"That's a shame but I believe it." I shook my head. "I went to a law school conference in Portland, Maine, last year and that exact same thing happened to me. It was downright scary."

We shared a good laugh.

"This is kind of scary to me, Patricia, but it's the good kind of scary." She walked into the Karibu bookstore and I followed her. "It feels great to be around so many of my people."

Oh, brother, I thought to myself. She's really trippin'. "I'm glad you feel at home here but don't be too trusting of people just because they look like you," I stated, feeling a warning was in order. I had heard all of the horror stories about innocent victims moving to a big city from the country only to be taken advantage of, abused, or even murdered. And frankly, Mary Ann seemed like a prime candidate for any and all of the above. "A lot of terrible things can happen in the city, especially when someone picks up on the fact that a person is naive."

Mary Ann looked like she was about to cry, putting a book on African-American history back on the shelf. "I'm not as naive as I look, Patricia. Just because I grew up differently than you doesn't make me an imbecile."

"That's not what I was implying!" I quickly replied, defending my words and feeling guilty because that's exactly what I was thinking.

She returned to browsing the books. "This is amazing. I had no idea that there were this many books written by and about African-Americans."

"Well, now you know."

"I want to stop back by here before we leave so I can buy a couple. But I don't want to have to lug them around the whole mall."

"Cool." I headed back out into the mall. "There's a lingerie store right down there. Want to check it out?"

"Lingerie? You mean panties?"

Like duh! "Yes, panties and other things. The great part is that they have underwear that actually fits the sistahs, unlike most lingerie stores."

"Sure, we can check it out," she agreed hesitantly, like she was almost too shy to look at undergarments with another woman peeking over her shoulder. The sistah was suffering from serious sexual oppression.

We were halfway into the store when she froze in place. I followed her ballooned eyeballs and spotted the point of interest. There were a couple of brothas walking out of the athletic-wear store directly across the way and they were F-O-I-N-E.

"See something you like, Mary Ann?" I asked teasingly.

"Uh, ye-ye-yes," she uttered. "Those men over there look good."

"Hell yeah, they look good and they probably taste good too." I nudged her in the side with my elbow and she blushed. "You ever suck a man's dick, Mary Ann?"

Her mouth fell open. "How dare you ask me something like that?"

I felt bad about asking but pursued the line of questioning anyway. "It's just that you seem a little inexperienced. Are you?"

"Absolutely not!" She took a step back and threw her hands on her hips. "I already told you all about Clarence."

"You told me he was your man back in South Dakota but I don't recall oral sex being broached in the discussion."

"Why should it be?" She bypassed the lingerie store and headed on down the mall, trying to get away from me.

I trailed her and got all in that ass. "Mary Ann, lack of sexual experience is nothing to be ashamed of. You just need to loosen up and live a little."

"I'm living just fine, thank you."

I grabbed her elbow, forcing her to stop. "Okay, I'm sorry. Are you hungry? I'm starved."

Her bottom lip was trembling. "I'm a little bit hungry. That cafeteria food on campus leaves a lot to be desired."

"That's putting it nicely." We both cackled. "Come on, they have an eatery down here in the center of the mall. We can sample a little bit of everything, Mexican, Chinese, and some bomb-ass fried chicken and throw down."

"Sounds good." She giggled.

● ● ●

We got our food and sat down at a table. It wasn't that crowded for a Sunday afternoon because most of the stores were about to close. Lo and behold, the same two brothas from earlier appeared out of nowhere and sat down at a table about fifty feet from us.

I realized I was about to push the limits of my new friendship. However, nothing beats a fail but a try. "Mary Ann, you see those same guys over there from earlier?"

"Yes, I noticed them," she replied nonchalantly.

"You want me to ask them to come over here and join us?"

"Whatever for?" she asked anxiously. "We don't know them."

"But we can get to know them." She kept glancing over there and almost fell out when one of them waved at her. "That one just waved at you. Want me to go get him for you?"

"No, no way," she muttered. "I don't want to seem desperate."

"Desperate? By picking up a guy in a mall? Chile, please, sistahs do it every day. I have picked up men everywhere, even on the street."

"Really?" Her eyes lit up like firecrackers. "I would never have the nerve to do something like that."

"If you ever plan to get a date around here, you better loosen up, gurlfriend. Competition around here is fierce. After you exclude all the ones in prison, the homosexuals, and the ones with jungle fever, decent black men are scarce. You have to find dick action where you can find it."

She almost choked for real that time on a piece of sweet-and-sour chicken. "It's not all about sex for me."

"So I figured."

"Besides, I would feel guilty being with someone else so soon after Clarence."

The two brothas chowed their food down in a matter of minutes, typical of the eating habits of men, and got up to empty their trays. The same one that was checking Mary Ann out earlier lingered around the trash bin for a few seconds to see if she was going to give him a green light to approach. When she pretended to be enthralled in her fried chicken wing, he and his buddy began to walk off.

"Last call for dick," I chided.

She threw her head back in laughter but I could tell she was faking.

We finished our meal and went back to Karibu so she could pick up a couple of novels. After that, we headed over to Green-belt Plaza to see *Sugar Hill* at the theater. Mary Ann commented on the *blackness* of the mall, assuming PG Plaza must have been a one-hit wonder.

We enjoyed the film and then headed back to campus. Before we said good night, I surveyed the array of roses in her room and issued one last warning. "Mary Ann, I'm not sure what your intentions are with Trevor but you really better watch your back."

"Can you please just answer me one thing?" she pleaded. I nodded. "You promise to answer honestly?"

I shrugged. "Sure, go ahead."

"You and Trevor have a past, don't you?"

I sucked in air and cupped my elbows. "Yes, he and I have a brief past. I fell for his shit and shinola just like the rest of the women our first year here."

"Do you still care about him?"

I guffawed. "No, you could *definitely* say that I don't care about him."

"I see." She sat down on her bed, picked up an envelope and pulled out a small note, undoubtedly a pussy plea from Trevor.

"Well, I'm about to do some studying and turn in." I opened her door and went out in the hallway.

"Yeah, me too."

"Cool. Good night."

"Good night."

I went into my room and opened a textbook but my mind was wandering. I couldn't tell Mary Ann what to do but I knew that Trevor wouldn't turn out to be everything she thought he was. That is, if she decided to date him. I hoped like all hell she wouldn't.

5

mary ann

I was torn three ways, between my loyalty to Patricia, my loyalty to Clarence, and my undeniable attraction to Trevor Ames. I wondered why he affected me so. Maybe it was because no one of his stature and sophistication had pursued me before. I would go eat my meals ten minutes before the kitchen closed, hoping to avoid him altogether. Then, I discovered that he rarely ate in the dining hall, so that was a relief. Apparently, he had been there the first day only to speak to his old friends.

We didn't have any classes together since he was in his last year, but I spotted him several times over the next few weeks in the courtyard. He was always flanked by this woman or that woman and I even saw him with FeFe one day having what looked like an intimate conversation under an elm. I couldn't figure him out. The flowers had finally stopped, as I knew they would. They must have set him back a pretty penny. But the notes still came.

He even had some nerdy-looking fellow serenade me one night. I almost went into convulsions from laughter. The guy stood below my window on Trevor's behalf strumming on a banjo and singing "You Light Up My Life." Trevor was mackin me hard, as they say. I was determined not to give in though. As long as I could successfully avoid him, I knew I could resist.

My luck ran out one Friday afternoon.

I was trying out a new facial mask I bought from a vendor across the street from the campus front gates. It was some cucumber–aloe-vera cream concoction that felt really cool against my skin but extremely tight. I had slapped it on after I had taken a shower and washed my hair. I had on a flannel bathrobe, my favorite fluffy slippers, and a towel wrapped around my head. There was a light tapping on my door. I swung the door open, assuming it was Patricia.

"Trevor!" I exclaimed, shocked to find him standing there looking as fine as ever. "Oh, my goodness! What are you doing here?"

"I came by to see my favorite girl." He handed me a huge bouquet of roses. "Since you won't answer my phone calls, I decided to drop these flowers off in person."

"Phone calls? What phone calls?" I feigned ignorance. I knew he had been ringing the pay phone off the hook. One sistah down the hallway was so disgusted with me one night, she threatened physical violence if I didn't call him back. "I don't have a phone."

"I've been calling you on the pay phone. Leaving messages with people. Several of them. You didn't get any of them?"

"Nope, not a one," I lied again. "Listen, I'm not presentable at the moment." I pulled the roses up close to my chest, realizing my nipples were hard like they always are as soon as I get out of the shower. "I'll call you later. I promise."

"I really need to talk to you. It won't take but a second and, besides, I've already seen you." He looked me up and down, making me feel uncomfortable. "You look stunning as usual."

"Very funny." I let him in the room and I headed into the bathroom. "I'll be right back. Just let me take this gook off my face." I hurriedly removed the mask with a warm wet towel and then brushed my teeth before going back out. "There. That's better." Trevor was flipping through a photo album on my bookshelf and then picked up the doll my little sister gave me when I left home. I was so ashamed. "So, what's going on?"

He set the doll back down, thank goodness. "I was lucky enough to snatch up a pair of tickets for the Dance Theater of Harlem tonight. I was wondering if you would do me the honor of attending with me."

"The Dance Theater of Harlem?" I asked excitedly. I had only seen their performance on the PBS channel back home several times. I marveled at how beautiful the dancers were. "The *real* one?"

"Yes, the *real* one." Trevor chuckled, probably wondering if I had lost my mind. "What do you think? That they have some generic version of it touring the country?"

"No, of course not." I tightened the bathrobe around my midsection, wishing I had some clothes on. "Silly me."

"It starts at eight sharp at the Kennedy Center so I'll pick you up about seven. Cool?"

He was mighty sure of himself but I must admit that it turned me on. I reminded myself that I was only asking for trouble if I accepted his invitation. "Um, thanks for the offer, Trevor, but—"

"Oh, come on, Mary Ann. Don't do this to me." He covered his heart with his right hand. "My poor heart can't take any more of your rejection."

"It's not that. I appreciate all the flowers and notes and attention but—"

"How hard does a brotha have to try with you to get a date?" He held up the index finger on his left hand. "Just one date?"

I tried to think of a viable excuse not to go. "I thought you were seeing FeFe?"

"FeFe is a friend. That's it." He walked up so close to me that I could smell his breath mint. "I'm only romantically interested in one woman at the moment." He ran his finger down the middle of my bathrobe and started moving toward my right nipple. "Guess who that is."

"I'm sorry but I must decline your offer," I uttered, jumping out of his path.

"May I ask why?"

"Because I still have feelings for someone back home." I wasn't sure how true that statement was but I did care about

Clarence. It wasn't love though. That much I was sure of. The passion died inside of me when I left him behind in South Dakota.

"Ouch!" He frowned. "Why not just rip my heart out and stomp on it?"

"I'm sure you'll have no problem finding a date for tonight." I sat down on my bed and picked up a pillow, still trying to cover my nipples, even though his actions a few seconds earlier meant he had already spotted them. "The women around here seem crazy about you."

"No, I think I'll just stay around the house tonight and mope. Maybe drink myself into a stupor and fall asleep fantasizing about you." He sighed heavily and then sat down beside me. I willed myself to show some self-control. "It's become a common occurrence."

"I'm really sorry, Trevor."

"Forget it." He hung his head like he was seriously hurt. "I guess I'll leave you alone now since you hate me."

"I don't hate you."

He stood up, reached into his jacket pocket, and pulled out a card, handing it to me. "If you should happen to change your mind, here's my number."

I looked at the card and couldn't believe he had embossed cards made up with his name, home phone number, and e-mail address on them. "Thanks, but my decision's final."

He sulked as he walked out the door. "I'm sorry to hear that."

• • •

My mind kept wandering to Clarence that afternoon. So much so that I decided to give him a call. We had written each other quite a few times but had only spoken once or twice.

His phone was snatched up on the first ring. "Hello? Hello?"

I was stunned to hear a female voice on the other end and entertained the thought that I might have misdialed, but I've always been a whiz at numbers. Besides, Clarence and I had been together for so long that I knew his number like the back of my hand. "Who is this?" I whispered cautiously into the phone.

"Who is this?" the female hissed back at me. There was a brief silence before she added, "Mary Ann, is that you?"

"Yes. Who the hell is this?" The fact that this heifer knew my name pissed me off so I got loud.

"It's me, Jessica." She giggled into the phone.

"Jessica?" Jessica Williams was my arch rival. I couldn't stand her. Mainly because she had never made any bones about wanting Clarence. She tried everything within her power to get him to bed her down but he had always refused her. "What are you doing answering Clarence's phone?"

"He's in the shower at the moment." *No, she didn't say he was in the damn shower?* "Hello? Mary Ann? You still there?" she said while I took all this in.

"So I take it you and Clarence are an item now?" I asked rhetorically, not wanting to believe it was actually happening. It wasn't so much that he had moved on as it was that he had moved on with that tramp.

"Something like that," she cackled into the phone. "I mean, you didn't want him. You threw him away. Personally, I think that makes you a damn fool but it's all the better for me."

"Bitch!" I wanted to climb through the phone line like that serial killer in *Shocker* and beat the shit out of her.

"Now I finally have what I've wanted all along. You're clear across the country and there's not a damn thing you can do about it."

Her boasting grew real tired real quick. "Tell Clarence to go to hell!" I screamed into the phone before slamming it back on the cradle.

I sat there for a few minutes in the old-fashioned phone booth with the sliding door closed for privacy, covering my face with my hands and fighting back tears. Then I decided two could play that game and went back to my room to find Trevor's playa card.

"Patricia, you in there?" I rapped loudly on her door.

"Hey, what's up, gurl?" she asked, yanking it open.

"I need a favor. Well, two actually."

"Sure. What do you need?"

"I need to borrow a dress." I walked into her room. "Something fancy."

"Aw, sounds like you have a hot date," she prodded.

"I don't know about hot but I have one with Trevor."

"I see." Her whole attitude immediately changed.

"I won't go if you prefer," I offered, feeling guilty. "I can call him right back and tell him all bets are off."

"No, it's cool," she replied despondently. "I guess some people just have to learn the hard way." I refused to comment before the situation turned ugly. "So where is he taking you, other than to his place to check out his *water bed?*"

"I have no intention of going to his place tonight or any other night!" I stated convincingly, which was no problem because I was dead serious on that point. I was planning on going out on one date with him to help get my mind off Clarence and that was it.

"Whatever, gurl." She rolled her eyes, crossed her arms, and smacked her lips. "Once he works his magic on you, you'll be begging him to take the drawers." I stood there debating whether to tell her off or just leave altogether. Gratefully, she saved me the trouble of doing either. "Never mind all that. Where are you going?"

"To see the Dance Theater of Harlem at the Kennedy Center."

She appeared genuinely stunned. "Trevor is really shelling out some cash on you. I hope you're ready to shell out some ass." I took a deep breath, upset that she would even imply such a thing. "I have this pretty little red number that would be perfect. Let me get it out of my closet."

"Thanks." I waited for her to riffle through her vast wardrobe and pull it out. It was an ankle-length strapless silk dress. I had only seen dresses like that in magazines. "It's beautiful."

"I think it will fit. I don't have any shoes that will fit you though. You look like you wear about a size seven shoe and I'm a nine."

"No problem. I have some shoes."

"I also have a red dinner jacket you can borrow. It might get chilly out tonight." I grinned at her, thankful that she was helping me. I definitely didn't have anything appropriate to wear nor could I afford to buy anything on such short notice. "So what's the other favor?"

"Can you help me look a little more presentable?" I asked, embarrassed that I felt I couldn't do it alone. "I mean, with my hair and makeup?"

Patricia laughed at me and retrieved her makeup bag from her dresser. "Just call me Fairy Godmother Pat."

"I'm speechless," Trevor said, looking debonair in a black double-breasted suit and flamboyant tie.

"I hope that's a good sign?" I asked, as nervous as a whore in church.

"Definitely!" He walked up to me on the sidewalk in front of the door, wrapped his arms around me, and kissed me on the cheek. I instantly became overheated. "You look like a princess all dressed up like that."

"Thanks for the compliment." I pushed him away from me before my nipples got hard again and started protruding out of the tight dress.

"Shall we go?" He opened the passenger-side door of his Porsche 911 and guided me inside.

"Certainly," I replied, sinking back into the fine leather bucket seat while I waited for him to join me.

"This is the most beautiful place I have ever seen!" I proclaimed as we walked into the Kennedy Center. The atmosphere was breathtaking and the chandeliers almost blew me away.

"It's not half as beautiful as you." Trevor kissed me on my cheek again and I melted. "After the show, I'll have to take you out on the balcony so we can look over the Potomac River into Virginia."

"Sounds wonderful."

We stood in line to get some cocktails and I decided to try a gin and tonic, which was taking a walk on the wild side for me. Other than experimenting with Mad Dog 20/20 a few times in the pool hall, and my uncle Rod's moonshine during the holidays, I hadn't dabbled much in alcohol.

"Let's take our seats, Mary Ann." Trevor paid the bartender for our drinks and left a couple of ones in the tip glass. "The show is about to start."

"So, what did you think?" Trevor asked me as we stood on the balcony after the show. I was speechless the entire time because I had never imagined anything so creative and innovative. The music had been perfect, the dancers had been perfect, Trevor had held my hand the entire time and that had felt perfect.

"I think I'm living a fairy tale." I looked out over the Potomac River and the lights in Virginia were nothing short of incredible. "Going places and experiencing things I've only read about."

Trevor placed my jacket over my shoulders and then cradled me with his left arm. "Stick with me and there will be a lot of nights like this."

"Really?" I searched his eyes for an honest answer. "Part of me wants to believe that, Trevor."

"And the other part?"

"The other part is still unsure about your intentions," I answered, looking back out over the river. "I've heard so many negative things."

"Don't listen to them. Most people are just jealous." He lifted my chin, forcing me to gaze into his dark, bedroom eyes. "A lot of women like me. You know that, but I'm following my heart and I hope that you will too."

We shared our first kiss and it was warm and delightful. I pulled away when it felt like he was lingering in my mouth a little too long and intimately.

"Can we go back to my place?" His hard dick was pressing against me through our clothing.

I shook my head, determined to stand my ground. "No, it's too soon."

"I understand." He kissed me lightly on the forehead. "I better get you back to the dorm."

6

patricia

I couldn't stand the way Mary Ann was acting. It had been three weeks since Trevor had taken her to see the Dance Theater of Harlem and all she ever talked about was him. How he had taken her to fabulous restaurants, bought her romantic trinkets, and catered to her every whim. It was nauseating.

Something had to be done. Drastic times called for drastic measures. Although, I knew from the moment I first met Mary Ann that she was APF material. Or could be turned into APF material, at least.

The sorors weren't going to be happy about it, but, oh well. I thought it was time to expand the D.C. chapter. All of the other chapters across the country were growing by leaps and bounds, and a new chapter had been formed in Chicago. We needed to play catch-up so we would be strongly represented at the annual convention.

I tracked Mary Ann down on a bench outside the student union, looking like she was floating on air. I wanted to ask her if she had given up the pussy to Trevor yet but I knew she would pitch a hissy fit. I didn't want Trevor for myself, after all, but he had hurt my feelings when I first started law school. I came full of hope of getting not only a great education but also a great man. He was the first one to show me some attention, kind of the same scenario as with Mary Ann. In my case it turned out that he wanted only to fuck me and then tell me to get a life.

Two years in APF had made a world of difference in my life. Olive found me and made me a real woman. She taught me the difference between love and sex and how both could exist in a woman's life without ever coinciding. Joining APF was the best thing I had ever done, and even though I wasn't seriously dating a man at the time, I had the most awesome sex at my beck and call. I was living large and it was time for Mary Ann to start living large too.

"Mary Ann, what's up, gurl?"

"Hey, Patricia!" She gazed up at me, flashing a perfect grin. "Just doing a little studying. It's chilly out but it's still a beautiful day so I thought I would take advantage of it. I get sick of studying in my room and in the library all of the time."

"I can dig it." I sat down on the bench beside her, moving a couple of her textbooks over. Just the sight of the antitrust law book sent chills up my spine. I hated that class when I took it. "I was wondering what you have planned for this weekend."

"Nothing much. Trevor is going home to see his folks."

Oh boy! Her whole life had begun to revolve around Trevor. "Well, that's a good thing."

"Why is that?" She asked the question with an edge of sarcasm in her voice.

"Whoa, there's no reason to get defensive about Trevor around me." I patted her on the knee. "You're a grown woman and I respect your decisions."

"I'm glad you do." She shut the book she was reading and closed her composition book. "What's going on this weekend?"

"I belong to this all-female investment club and I was wondering if you wanted to sit in on our monthly meeting Saturday."

"Investment club!" She laughed in my face. "I barely have two nickels to rub together, much less money to invest in the stock market or whatever it is you all invest in."

"We invest in different things and, trust me, you don't need a lot of money to get your foot in the door." I began to rethink my actions. I wasn't sure inviting her without consulting the others was fair.

"How much money do you need?"

Her interest seemed genuinely piqued. However, if she'd known the real deal, she would've run for the hills. "Twenty, thirty dollars a month," I replied, shrugging my shoulders. "Whatever you can afford to pitch in. Your return is based on your initial investment."

"So let me get this straight. You combine your finances and invest in things and then split the profits?"

"We don't really touch the profits," I stated honestly. "That defeats the purpose. The real money is in long-term investments but our portfolio is extremely versatile."

"Sounds cool."

Cool? She was getting hip and everything! "Yes, it is cool. So, you interested?"

"Maybe, but what about the other women in the club? Do you think they'll mind?"

"No, not at all." I was lying my ass off. I would be lucky if Olive didn't slap the shit out of me on sight. "They always welcome new members."

"How many of you are there?"

"Twelve."

"That's a small group."

"Yes, but we belong to a larger group."

"Really?"

I knew I was going a little bit too far so I just said, "I'll explain that all to you later. So, are you down or not?"

She started pulling on her gloves. The wind had picked up in a matter of moments and it was turning chilly. "Sure, why not? I don't have anything else to do Saturday with Trevor going out of town and all."

I turned my head so she couldn't see me rolling my eyes. "Wonderful." I looked back at her. "We'll leave about two, okay?"

"Okay." I got up to leave. "What about a dress? Is this one of those fancy type of meetings?"

"No, not really." I suppressed a laugh, wondering how she would react if we fell up in there and everyone was buck naked playing with dildos. That never happened at investment club meetings though. We were strictly business. "Just wear whatever you feel comfortable in."

"Okay." I was about thirty feet away when she yelled out at me. "Thanks for inviting me!"

I snickered, anxious for Saturday to get there so I could see what would become of my dirt. "Oh, you're so very welcome, Mary Ann. Don't mention it."

7

olive

I was hoping the investment meeting didn't go over the two hours allotted for it that day. We hadn't started the meeting yet because Patricia was running late, and I was ready for the chicas to get out my crib already. I needed to get to the beauty parlor by six to get my hair done for a medical society benefit I was attending that night. I was hoping to hit Georgetown Park Mall long enough to pick up a new dress as well. Plus, I was suffering from PID (Pussy in Distress).

I'm a plastic surgeon and it had been a long week at the office. Mad women had simultaneously felt the urge to get something nipped and tucked or implanted. There was a plastic surgery boom those days. The trend began in the late nineteen eighties and had grown twofold by the nineties. I was happy as shit about it too. The more people that were unhappy with their appearance, the more money in my pocket.

People, in particular my parents, always bombarded me with questions about why I chose to become a plastic surgeon instead of a cardiologist or neurologist. I knew what the deal was when a few of my friends in college opted to get silicone injections instead of stuffing their bras with toilet tissue and socks. I mean, after all, eventually the clothes have to come off and no man wants to suck on a pair of sweat socks.

Anyway, back to my PID issue. I hadn't had sex in five days—a long-ass time when you like to get your freak on as much as I do. My boyfriend Hakim worked for a large computer corporation based out of Hong Kong and spent a lot of time overseas. In fact, it was just as well that Hakim and I didn't see each other much because it meant I had more time for Drayton.

Hakim was a sensible relationship while Drayton was strictly a fuck thing. In fact, he never even knew my real name the entire time we were fucking the shit out of each other. I never brought him over to my place and he had no idea what I did for a living. He just knew I loved to fuck and as far as I was concerned, that's all his ass needed to know.

Hakim, on the other hand, knew everything about me. He had even flown home with me to San Francisco on several occasions to see my folks. He was the type of man I could take to social gatherings, the type of man I could justify a serious relationship with, and the type of man that could afford me. Not that I can't afford my own luxuries but why should I work my ass off while a man sits at home on the couch all day? D.C.

has tons of fine-ass men but a lot of them bad boys are hanging on the corner day and night. That's just not for me.

I peeped at the time on the clock Hakim bought for me in Switzerland that stood on my mantel. It was a quarter to four. Where the hell was Patricia? I was just about to poll the sorors to see if any of them knew her whereabouts when the doorbell rang. Bout damn time!

I was all set to get into Patricia's ass when I swung the door open, but my mouth fell open instead. The chica had shown up with someone else in tow. Before I could regain my composure, Patricia ran up to me, embraced me, and whispered in my ear. "Don't have a hissy fit. I can explain."

I threw on a factitious smile and eyed the sistah in my doorway up and down. She looked more nervous than a virgin in a whorehouse. She was attractive. And trust me, I know attractive features. They are my bread and butter. She had these huge, sparkling brown eyes; full, luscious lips; naturally curly, shoulder-length brown hair; and a body some women would cut their right arm off for.

"Hey, Olive, sorry we're late," Patricia said loudly, letting the other women in my place know she had arrived and wasn't alone. I heard whispers coming from the living room. Yvette peeked her head around the corner to see what was going on and then quickly disappeared so she could issue a full report to the others. "Olive, this is Mary Ann Ferguson," Patricia said, pointing to her friend who was sporting a dress I'd seen Patricia wearing on more than one occasion. "Mary Ann, this is Olive—"

I jumped in before she could blurt out my *real* last name. "Cox," I stated. "My name is Olive Cox."

This Mary Ann chica laughed, not overlooking the irony of my pseudonym.

She proffered her hand. "Nice to meet you, Olive Cox."

I shook it but refrained from saying it was nice to meet her because it wasn't. I was too busy wondering if Patricia had lost her damn mind. I could tell in the span of one sentence that the sistah was a country bumpkin and country bumpkins and I had never mixed. That's why I try to avoid my family reunions in North Cackalaky as much as I can.

"Come on in." Patricia brushed past me into the living room with the black Tammy Wynette in tow. "Let me introduce you to the others."

"Umm, Patricia," I called after her, muttering some expletives underneath my breath. "Can I see you in my bedroom for a moment?"

"Everyone, this is Mary Ann," I heard her announce. "Mary Ann, this is everybody. Please introduce yourselves, sistahs."

Even from my vantage point, I could tell no one was saying a word. "Patricia, we need to talk. *Now!*"

"I'll be right back, Mary Ann," she told her protégée. "Just have a seat wherever you like and help yourself to the refreshments."

"Thanks," I heard the country bumpkin reply. "Hello, everyone."

Still, no one said a word and I didn't blame them.

I waited for Patricia in my bedroom, and once she entered, I closed the door. "How dare you bring that countrified chica up in my place?" I laid into her ass.

"Olive, calm down," she snickered. "Mary Ann's cool people."

I crossed my arms in front of me and rolled my eyes up to the ceiling. "Mary Ann! What an Arcadian-sounding name. I bet her daddy owns a pig farm down in Tennessee!"

Patricia fell out laughing and plopped down on my king-sized bed. "Actually, her dad raises chickens in South Dakota."

I knew it! She had *Hee Haw* written all over her ass! "Patricia, what's so damn funny? I'm not the least bit amused by any of this. I know the rest of the sorors are out there sitting on pins and needles."

"I don't see why they would be." She picked up the latest edition of *Essence* off my nightstand and started flipping through an article they had on African-American bachelors. "It's only our investment club meeting."

"It's only our investment club meeting, It's only our investment club meeting," I repeated, mocking her. "We all made an agreement that *no one* would bring someone up in here without the sorority discussing it first."

Patricia smacked her lips in disgust. "I just wanted to introduce her around. How can they discuss someone they've never met?"

I sat down at my vanity and applied another coat of mocha lipstick. My first coat was out there somewhere on a wine glass.

"Olive, it's not like this is freak night," Patricia protested. "There's not a dick in the house."

I looked at her reflection in the mirror. "That's not the point and you know it. Besides, from what I've seen so far, that chica's scared of her own shadow, much less a dick."

Patricia giggled again, irritating me all the more. "I'm telling you that Mary Ann has potential. She just needs to loosen up a bit. She's not too keen on strangers."

"So what's she supposed to do on freak nights?" I asked sarcastically. "Shiver under the covers?"

"See, now you're being damn ridiculous!" Patricia hissed at me. "APF may not be the right thing for her. I'll concede that much, but I'd like to nominate her anyway. There's only one way to find out whether she's down or not."

"You're forgetting one thing," I swiftly reminded her. "Our membership is closed. We voted to keep the D.C. membership to an even dozen. Remember?"

"Let's make it a baker's dozen then."

My PID flared up again. "Miss Hee Haw isn't APF material and that's the bottom freakin' line!"

Patricia slammed the magazine shut and threw it down on my black satin bedspread. "They all said the same thing about me at first but you fought tooth and nail to get me inducted."

She had a valid point but that was a totally different situation. When I first met Patricia at an art gallery opening, I knew she was APF material from jump street. "That's because I sensed something remarkable about you."

"Well, I sense something remarkable about Mary Ann."

I ran a brush through my *good* hair and smudged my eyebrow pencil in a little better. "I can't imagine what."

"You've spent all of two minutes with her." Patricia got up off the bed, walked over to me, picked up the brush off the vanity and started brushing my hair for me. "Give her a chance. That's all I'm asking. For me. Please!"

She knew that little puppy dog pout always lured me in. I could never deny her anything. After all, she was my master-piece. "Okay, fine! I'll go out there and see what she's talking about, where her head is, but I'm not promising anything."

"I understand." Patricia beamed, glad I had given in. "Thanks, soror!"

"Hmph, all I can say is this: You better not show up at our little soiree in a couple of weeks with the chicken farm queen in tow, or else."

"Or else what?"

"You'll find out." I tried to sound serious but almost cracked a smile.

"Aw, save your idle threats, Olive. You might stress some people out but you could never intimidate me." She put the brush back down and finished up her styling with her fingers. I had to admit Patricia could work wonders with a do and skip-ping my six o'clock hair appointment had suddenly become a feasible option. "Underneath that fire-and-ice exterior, I know you're just a puddy cat."

I got up from my vanity bench. "Let's just go back out to check on the others. I bet they're being so quiet, you can hear the kitchen faucet dripping."

"Thanks for giving Mary Ann a chance." Patricia gave me a huge bear hug and I was hoping she wouldn't mess up my do after she just hooked it up. "She's smart, she's attractive, and she has an extremely bright future in front of her."

"Yeah, and she's also from South Dakota," I stated with an edge of sarcasm in my voice. We walked back out into the living room and all the sorors looked shell-shocked while Miss Hee

Haw was in the dining room piling celery sticks and blue cheese dressing on one of my fine china plates. "See, I told you they'd be pissed off over this."

"Just call the meeting to order," Patricia whispered in my ear.

patricia

"Sorry about that." I joined Mary Ann at the dining room table and picked up a plate of my own. "I had to talk to Olive about something right quick. You having a good time?"

I could tell by the expression on Mary Ann's face that she wasn't. "Actually, I was thinking about waiting for you in the car. I don't fit in here. That's obvious."

"Yes you do." I found Olive's buffalo wings, my favorite, and put six of them on my plate. One thing about Olive: The sistah can put a hurting on some food. "You're here with me. Thus, you fit in. Just relax."

"I get the impression they don't want me here. No one said a word to me the entire time you were in the bedroom. They've just been in there staring at me and whispering to each other."

"Don't worry about it." No sooner had I responded than Olive called the meeting to order. I took Mary Ann's hand and led her into the living room. "Let's just have a seat."

The meeting went well, all things considered. While none of the sorors acknowledged each other by their names, real or imagined, we managed to get some business done and our investment portfolio was up three percent from the previous month.

Olive kept staring across the room at Mary Ann, undoubtedly sizing up her APF potential. Without question, Mary Ann was uncomfortable, but I wanted her there just the same. In time, I knew she would win them all over if they only gave her the opportunity.

After the official business was over, the sorors cleared out of there like women headed to the day-after-Thanksgiving sale at Best Buy. The entire place was empty in a matter of seconds, leaving just Olive, Mary Ann, and me gazing at each other in silence.

"So, Mary Ann, you go to school with Patricia?" Olive's voice was full of disdain. "She says you're very smart."

"Yes, she and I live in the same dorm," Mary Ann replied hesitantly.

"How long have you been in D.C.?"

"Just a couple of months."

"How do you like it?"

"I have enjoyed myself so far. Patricia has been kind enough to show me around."

Olive threw a look at me that I couldn't quite make out the origin of and then continued with her interview. That's exactly what she was up to, interviewing Mary Ann for APF without her even suspecting it.

"I understand you're from South Dakota?"

"Yes, born and raised," Mary Ann stated proudly. I had noticed she didn't seem as ashamed of her upbringing as she was when I first met her. "I love the country. I won tons of medals in the junior rodeo competitions."

"How impressive," Olive replied, not meaning it for one second. "There must not be much to do in South Dakota, other than raising chickens, huh?"

It was Mary Ann who glared at me that time. "I see Patricia has told you a lot about me."

"Not really," Olive replied snidely. "Just where you are from and what your family does for a living."

Mary Ann took Olive and me both off guard with her next string of questions. In fact, I almost spit out my wine all over my blouse.

"I take it the two of you were discussing me in detail in your bedroom? Is that what you needed to talk to Patricia about? Am I not welcome here in your home?"

I could tell by the way Olive's mouth frowned up that she was about to cop a serious attitude. "Don't flatter yourself, chica. You're of absolutely no importance to me. However, I have to be honest with you. Our investment club meetings are usually handled with a great degree of privacy and I was a bit offended when Patricia showed up with you unexpectedly."

Mary Ann stood up and headed for the door. "Patricia, can we please go now?" I stared at Olive, waiting for her to issue an apology. "If not, I'll just meet you down in the car or I can catch the bus back to campus." She put her hands on her hips and leered at Olive. "Is there a bus stop around here, Miss High-and-Mighty?"

Olive jumped to her feet. "What did you just call me?"

"You heard me!"

"Look, this is not the day to be fucking with me, all right!" Olive blared. That's when I knew she must've had that daggone PID she was always complaining about. Hakim must've been on a business trip. "This is my home and I won't have you talking to me like that up in here!"

Yep, it was definitely the PID. She was starting to sound ghetto and Olive hated sounding ghetto. She would only slip when she was sexually frustrated.

Mary Ann was about to issue a comeback but I jumped all in the mix. "That's enough, you two." I walked over to the front door. "Let's go, Mary Ann. Maybe this wasn't such a good idea after all."

"You can say that again," Olive sneered at me.

Mary Ann walked out in the hallway and waited for me. I closed the door just long enough to issue my objections to Olive. "You didn't have to be so mean!"

"She copped an attitude first," Olive whined.

"No, everything was kosher until you started poking fun at her background. You ought to be ashamed of yourself. You weren't exactly raised with a silver spoon in your mouth either." I knew that would get her. As much as she tried to hide it, Olive came from very humble beginnings and was the first person in her family to attend college. "I'm leaving because I don't want to be rude and leave Mary Ann lingering in the hallway. You and the rest of the sorors have been rude enough."

"We'll continue this discussion later, Patricia."

"We damn sure will," I said, before storming out.

8

mary ann

"You know, baby, we've been dating for quite some time now?" Trevor commented while we finished up the dinner dishes in his town house.

"Yes, we have," I agreed.

"And I've tried to show you how much I care about you." He dried the last dish and pulled the stopper out of the sink so the water could drain. "Do you believe I care about you?"

"It seems like you do." I knew exactly where our conversation was headed. He wanted some sex and I had been holding out on him big time.

"I do." He wrapped his strong arms around my waist and flicked his tongue across my lips. "My feelings for you are undeniable."

"I care about you too, Trevor."

He ran the fingers of his left hand through my hair and then proceeded to lay a long, wet kiss on me. "Enough to finish the feelings?"

"Trevor, I don't know what to say." I really didn't know what to say. I did want him, but I was afraid that once he got what he wanted, my ass would be history just like all the others.

"Say that you'll be with me tonight." He took my right hand and kissed the inside of my palm. That was one of my weak spots. "That you'll stay here and wake up tomorrow morning in my arms."

"Is that what you really want?" I lovingly gazed up into his eyes.

"Nothing would make me happier." He started massaging my shoulders. I'm sure he knew I was nervous. I was always nervous when we discussed sex. "I understand your apprehensions but I can assure you that this is real."

"Can we just wait a little while longer?" I pleaded, even though I was more than ready for him to jump my bones. For the previous three weeks or so, I had been masturbating on a daily basis, something I had never done before I met him.

He took a deep, restorative breath. "If you insist, but I'm a man, Mary Ann. Men have needs."

"I recognize that."

"I don't know how much longer I can hold out."

"What is that supposed to mean?" I asked with an edge of sarcasm in my voice. "That if I don't give it up, you're going to get it elsewhere?"

"No, that's not what I meant." He threw his hands in the air.

"Then what?" I insisted.

"Let's just sit here by the fire and relax." He guided me into the living room and urged me to sit down on the hearth by his gas fireplace. "You want some more wine?"

"Yes, please." He picked up our glasses from the coffee table and went back into the kitchen.

While he was gone, I debated about the timing. I was sick of missing out on sex. I still harbored some subtle feelings for Clarence, but nothing major. He had written me to apologize about Jessica answering his phone that day, claiming nothing had happened. Bullshit and I knew it. That's why I refused to return any of his calls or respond to his mail. Trevor was there for me, and while I wasn't positive his motives were genuine, he'd shown me a good time and taken me places no other man had. Maybe he deserved a little something special in return.

"Here you go." He handed me a glass full of red wine and broke my trance.

"Thanks."

He sat down beside me and we started kissing again, this time more heavily. When we came up for air, he contradicted his actions. "I don't want to pressure you."

"Good." I took a sip of wine and let the jazz music playing on the CD vibrate through my body.

"If it's okay with you, can we just sleep together tonight? In my bed?" He started rubbing my knee. I was glad I had on leggings because I assumed he would have moved his hand north if I had had on a dress. He was a little rough when I had let him finger me before, but the feeling was different. I enjoyed it. "We don't have to do anything. Not unless you want to."

"I'll think about it." My panties were getting damp and I knew I was on the brink of giving it up. "Can I ask you something?"

"You can ask me anything you like."

"Why are you so infatuated with me?"

"Honestly?"

"I asked, didn't I?"

"Because of your innocence."

I laughed. "My innocence?"

"Yes. I can tell you're not very experienced and that turns me on. Men use hoes, they don't settle down and marry them."

"You're wild." I laughed.

"No, just trying to keep it real." He took my glass and set it down on the hearth along with his and gathered my hands into his, gazing directly into my eyes. "I'm in my last year of law school and some of the top firms in the country are already pursuing me. While many of the offers are tempting, I plan to stay right here in the metropolitan area. It's my home now."

"I like it here too," I concurred. D.C. had turned out to be much more than I expected. I had even started hanging out at a few nightclubs around town, with and without Trevor. Sometimes I went with Patricia, other times I caught a cab and went by myself. I especially enjoyed reggae clubs. I loved the way people moved their bodies to the music.

"The way I see it, there is only one vital part of my life missing." Trevor tightened his grip on my hands. "A good woman. Someone I can take home to my parents in Indiana and be proud to call mine."

"And you think I'm that person?"

"I know you are." He started kissing my fingertips one at a time. First my left hand and then the right one. "How many men have you ever been with?"

Part of me wanted to lie, but honesty prevailed. "I've only gone all the way with one."

"I rest my case." He chuckled. "I need you in my life. I'm not talking marriage right off the bat. We could wait until you graduate, but I could help to support you and things like that."

"I would like that." I wasn't sure where I wanted my relationship with Trevor to go but it seemed like the appropriate response at the moment.

"So will you consider it? Becoming my woman officially?"

"What about all the women you've bedded down?"

"It's different for men. Men are expected to sow their wild oats and live a little."

Now I was agitated. How unfair of men to think they can sleep with a hundred women and then come down on women who do the same. "So I'm just supposed to overlook all of that?"

"I can't change my past, Mary Ann. I can only prepare for the future and my future includes you."

We sat there by the fire talking for about another hour. When the grandfather clock in his foyer struck midnight, I told Trevor to take me to bed.

We made love, if that's what you want to call it. He blew my earlobe. That didn't turn me on because his breath was kind of tart. He fondled and sucked my breasts for less than a minute before he was trying to get his dick inside of me. I really hadn't gotten wet yet so he had some problems manuevering it in. He finally managed but once it was in, he came in less than two

minutes after yelling out, "Damn, this is some good-ass pussy!"
It wasn't what I had built it up to be in my mind. Not hardly.
The foreplay was quick, the actual sex was even quicker, and he
was out like a light within thirty minutes. For a man who had
been through so many women and had supposedly broken so
many hearts, I was totally disappointed. I was expecting him to
"blow my mind."

As he slept soundly, I lay there with his head buried in my
chest, wondering if things would be better the next time. I sure
as hell hoped so.

9

mary ann

Boy, did Olive Cox and I get off on the wrong foot! All of Patricia's investment club members seemed to distance themselves from me. It couldn't have been my country accent because I barely got the chance to open my mouth. Even that sistah Yvette, the one that Patricia introduced me to in the dining hall, wouldn't give me the time of day.

I thought about getting Olive Cox's phone number from Patricia and calling her to apologize. I found it hard to believe that someone, anyone, would name their child that but I guess anything is possible. My parents didn't raise me to act a fool in other people's homes. I felt bad about my behavior. She was rude and obnoxious, but that didn't mean I had to return the favor. Two wrongs never make a right.

Just when I had almost forgotten about her, I spotted her one afternoon. I had caught a cab down to an eclectic area of the District called Adams Morgan. I had heard so much about it that my curiosity was sparked. It was a virtual melting pot within the city, just as I had heard. People from every country and nationality you could think of were walking down the streets. I saw my first Rastafarian that day. He was selling watches and other jewelry on one of the corners. He tried to convince me his fifteen-dollar necklaces were fourteen-karat gold but I didn't believe he would be selling real gold for that price. These days, I realize people sell even more impressive things than that on the street; especially when the goods are *hot*.

Just as I was walking out of an African clothing store, it started to pour. I stood in the shop's doorway for shelter, hoping the rainstorm would quickly pass so I could head on back to campus before dark. Two Hispanic women joined me under the awning and started speaking Spanish to one another. I couldn't make out a thing they were saying, which was a shame considering I took Spanish in junior high.

I saw a couple across the street coming out of the grocery store. The guy was tall with a head full of dreadlocks. I had never seen him before but I recognized the woman.

"Olive!" I shouted out. She didn't even turn in my direction, it was obvious she couldn't hear me over the rain. I tried again to no avail. "Olive!"

They made their way down the sidewalk on the opposite side of the street. I decided it was now or never to try to reconcile with her for my behavior. I left the covering and tried to shield my head with my backpack. I sprinted across the street, barely dodging a souped-up Chevy that was flying down the street. The driver tooted his horn and the group of teenage boys in the car starting whistling and yelling sexual innuendoes at me out the window.

I ignored them and searched for Olive and her companion who had gotten lost in the crowd. I continued in the direction they had been headed and was about to give up when I saw them about a hundred feet away turning a corner. She had her arm intertwined with his and I wondered if he was her lover.

I made it to the corner and hesitated when I realized it was an alleyway. It was dirty, concealed, and looked like something out of a gangster film. One of those alleys that people went down, never to be seen or heard from again.

I was about to turn around when I heard a woman giggling through the rain. I deduced it had to be Olive laughing and slowly walked deeper into the alley. There were two tall, brick apartment buildings, one on each side, and clothes were hanging on lines stretched from one side to the other, getting more soaked than they were when the tenants hung them up to dry.

I passed a trash Dumpster and almost jumped out of my skin when someone grabbed my ankle. I looked down and there was a homeless man—holding onto me. He flashed a toothless grin at me and with his free hand took a swig from a bottle of malt liquor.

"Please let go of me," I pleaded.

He let out this hideous laugh and then freed me.

I broke out in a run then, toward Olive and her friend. Looking back at it now, I'm not sure why I didn't run back the other way toward the crowded street. The drunken man scared me. So I was compelled to run toward someone who was familiar. Even if it was Olive. I wasn't thinking clearly in that moment.

I ran past an open door and backtracked when I heard Olive's voice. I went down some steps and followed the sound of her voice. They led into a dank basement of some sort.

"I had to see you today."

"Really? Why is that?" her male companion asked.

"That damn PID again." She giggled. Her friend started laughing. I wondered what she was talking about.

"Well, let's just see if we can do something about that," he said as I turned a corner and spotted them against a back wall.

Besides them the place was empty. The only light was coming from a couple of broken windows. Water gushing from a drainpipe was the only sound besides their voices.

I was about to speak when Olive grabbed the guy by the back of the head and pulled him closer to her, shoving her tongue into his mouth.

I was frozen in place, torn between saying something and leaving. But I was still too scared to go back out in the alley past that horrid man.

The couple didn't see me. They were too busy ripping each other's clothes off. They didn't completely undress but the guy pulled Olive's trench coat off her shoulders and then ripped the buttons off her blouse, exposing her bra. He reached into her bra and pulled one breast out, then the other. Then he pushed them together so he could suckle on them together.

I remained frozen in my tracks.

He picked Olive up and walked over to the drainpipe with her legs wrapped around his torso. Water cascaded down on the two as she pulled his sweatshirt out of the band of his jeans, up and over his head.

Olive opened her eyes for a second and I was sure I was cold busted but she quickly closed them again. She started moaning as the man licked her breast.

I was weak in the knees but found enough strength in my legs to take a few steps backward. I almost screamed as I felt some-thing run across my foot. A huge rat scampered away. Having grown up on a farm, I wasn't afraid of rats, so I relaxed. I was used to any type of rodent or animal imaginable, even snakes.

While I knew I had no business watching what happened next, I simply couldn't help myself. Olive unwrapped her legs from the man. Then he lifted her skirt up around her hips and ripped her satin panties off. He stayed down on his knees in front of her. Her back against a wall, she lifted one thigh up, then the other, onto his shoulders. He buried his head between her thighs.

This was the first time I had ever seen pussy-eating first-hand. Clarence and I had never ventured there. Trevor claimed he was going to, but in the three weeks of our sleeping together he had yet to back up his promises. This sex scene unfolding be-fore my eyes was such a turn-on that I let my backpack tumble to the ground. I began to caress my nipples between my thumbs and forefingers through my sweater.

Olive moaned louder and I got hornier. I couldn't take it anymore. I backed up against a wall, reached between my legs with my right hand, and rubbed my clit through my leggings.

I kept my eyes trained on the man and what he was doing to Olive. Then, I spotted it. I don't know when he released the monstrosity from his jeans but he did. It was the biggest dick I had ever seen anywhere. In person, in magazines, in porn flicks. Anywhere.

I started gasping for breath—and tried to refrain from moaning. I pulled the top of my leggings down with one hand so I could slip the other one down the front. I found my own wetness and started furiously rubbing myself, skin against skin.

At that point I stopped watching the two of them and shut my eyes. I got lost in my own little world of ecstasy and imagined the man doing such sensual things to me; to my body. I palmed my left breast with my free hand. Soon, I could feel cum trickling down onto my fingertips buried deep into the crotch of my pants.

Now, I let myself moan. I came like I never had before, forgetting all about Olive and her lover until . . .

I opened my eyes after I had exploded and they stood there together, her breasts and his dick exposed, glaring at me with disdain.

"I don't freakin' believe this shit!" Olive screamed. "What the fuck are you doing here?"

I pulled my hand out of my pants and struggled to find my tongue. "Olive, I'm so sorry. I didn't mean to . . ." I blurted out.

Olive walked over, grabbed me by my hair and started yanking it. I pushed her in the stomach. Her friend had followed her and lifted her up in the air, forcing her to let me go.

"Cynda, calm down," he instructed. He had the deepest, sexiest voice and he was gorgeous—even better looking up close. I had never been attracted to men with dreadlocks, the few I had seen. But he was all that. "Leave her be! And who is Olive?"

"Leave her be? Leave her be?" Olive said, kicking her legs up in the air, trying to break free from his grasp. "I'm going to kick her countrified ass!"

I yanked my backpack up from the ground and headed for the doorway, no longer concerned about the drunken bastard beside the Dumpster. "Please don't tell Patricia!" I yelled out as I turned the corner.

I ran down the alley and halfway back to campus before I slowed down. I found myself in a neighborhood I didn't recognize and parked myself at a bus stop, getting drenched while I caught my breath. A Metro bus headed to Union Station pulled up. I hopped on, got off at Union Station, and sat in the eatery nursing cups of hot cocoa for the remainder of the evening. I was too petrified to go back to campus and face Patricia. Olive was probably camped out in front of my door or, worse yet, across the hall in Patricia's room telling her everything.

Ultimately, when the eatery shut down I had to go back to campus. I was shaking like a leaf the entire cab ride back to the dorm. I scurried inside, ran up the back steps so I wouldn't meet anyone in the elevator, and hid in my room with the covers over my head. I finally managed to fall asleep around two in the morning, but not before I masturbated again. I came all over the sheets thinking about that sexy-ass man in dreads.

10

olive

"Damn," I hissed underneath my breath, glancing down at my silver Giorgio Armani watch. I had gotten Mary Ann's class schedule by going to the administration office and pretending it was a family emergency. I pretended to be her older sister and they fell for it. Dumb asses! It was well after three and her Antitrust Law class was running over schedule. It didn't matter though. I had no intention of leaving until I schooled her little country-bumpkin ass about a few things.

I started pacing up and down the marble hallway of the Marshall Memorial Building. The three-inch heels of my black leather pumps echoed loudly in the deserted corridor.

"Dammit, what's taking so long!" I was past frustrated and way past pissed. Thank goodness my academic years were behind me. No more sitting in cold auditoriums for this righteous sister, listening to boring-ass professors, and trying to stay awake.

After spending my residency eating Snickers bars from the vending machines for dinner and enduring thirty-six-hour shifts in the emergency room of D.C. General, my medical practice was finally beginning to take off. *That dues-paying shit is for the birds!*

My days of handling gunshot victims and stitching up stab wounds, dealing with trauma victims who didn't give a damn whether they lived or died themselves, and treating horny-ass prisoners from the D.C. jail who would rather get a quickie than medical treatment, were all a thing of the past.

Since then, I had hit pay dirt, dealing in tummy tucks and breast implants. I made a killing off people who refused to be satisfied with what nature gave them. Nothing beats having a successful medical practice. Well, almost nothing!

I leaned against the wall and grinned, reminiscing about the naughty things I did the day before. My plan had gone off as smooth as silk until Mary Ann's trifling, holier-than-thou ass showed up. How dare she invade my privacy like that? Granted, it was kind of an exposed area but her ass followed me and that shit simply wouldn't be tolerated.

There I was getting my freak da hell on, getting my pussy out of distress, fucking the daylights out of that ole boy, relieving some tension from dealing with Gladys Wallingford—a seventy-year-old patient who was convinced I could make her look twenty again—getting sexed out, when Little Miss Innocent reared her ugly head. I couldn't wait to get my hands on her ass.

While I waited my pantyhose started itching my inner thighs. I wished I had on thigh-high stockings so I could've easily slipped them bad boys off. It was hot as hell in D.C. for October, and it's a shame I even had to wear hose at all in that weather.

I inched my skirt up a little to scratch the itch, trying to be inconspicuous, and wouldn't you know it. I saw an ugly-ass bama with shaving bumps all over his damn face walking down the hall toward me, trying to get his peek on. I lowered my skirt and rolled my eyes, letting him know his ass better not even try to step to me. He walked past me, sucking on his teeth like I was a bucket of KFC before he continued on down the hall. He was all too obvious in turning around to size up my ass. Who gives a shit? I do have one hell of an ass.

The double doors to Auditorium C finally swung open and peeps started flying out of there like refugees from the Cambodian regime. I smirked, remembering all too well the feeling of relief I used to have once class let out.

Mary Ann was one of the last ones to exit class. She was walking with the professor, some man that looked old enough to be my great-great-great-grandaddy. It figured that she was trying to be the teacher's pet. She probably used to take apples to her elementary-school teachers and other country shit like that. "Mary Ann, can I have a word with you?"

She was stunned. "Umm, sure, Olive." She looked at her professor and forced a smile. "Thanks for helping me with those equations, Professor Wallington."

"No problem."

Mary Ann said nothing more until the professor and the rest of the students cleared out down the hall. I started to cold-bust her in front of everyone: ask her how it felt to play with her coochie while she was watching me fuck.

"What's up, Olive?" she finally asked, obviously on the brink of a nervous breakdown. "I'm surprised to see you here." I grabbed her by the arm and forced her back into the classroom. "What's wrong with you? Are you nuts?"

"Hell naw, I'm not nuts! Are you?" She feigned innocence but she was not even fooling me. "What in the hell did you think you were doing yesterday?"

"I—I—um."

"Yes?"

"I was just trying to say hello to you. I saw you on the street before you turned into the alley."

"Yeah, right," I snidely replied.

"Seriously," she professed. "I saw you coming out of a grocery store and I followed you down the alley so I could say hello. We had that little run in at your place before when I came to the meeting and I wanted to try to apologize, to bond with you."

"Bond with me?" Was this chica for real? "How is watching me get my freak on and masturbating trying to bond?"

Tears welled up in her eyes. "I'm so ashamed. Please don't tell Patricia. I wouldn't be able to look her in the face ever again."

I had her right where I wanted her. "You listen to me. Don't you ever spy on me again. If you're so sexually oppressed that you have to get yourself off while you watch another sistah get some, then that's a personal problem. Get your jollies off watching someone else."

Something changed in her facial expression and it was halfway scary. She got all up in my face. "You really think you're all that, don't you?"

"I know I'm all that," I replied cause dammit, I am.

"I wasn't turned on by watching you. It's not like you did anything earth-shattering. Even I can do better than that."

"Really?"

"Word up?"

Damn, she was beginning to talk like she was from the hood! "Then why were you over there digging your fingers all in your pussy?" I asked. "How come, huh? How come?"

"Because . . ."

"Because what?"

She backed away and sat down in one of the seats in the back row of the classroom. "Because I liked the way that guy was touching you."

"Remarkable," I whispered before I realized the word had even formed on my lips.

"What's remarkable?"

"Never mind." It dawned on me that she might be APF material after all. I still thought she was all shit and shinola though. There was only one way to get to the bottom of things. "So, you liked the way that ole boy was working me over, huh?" I tried to sound a tad more friendly.

"It was interesting." I sat down in the row in front of her and rotated my hips in the chair so I could face her. "He seemed very experienced."

"Would you like to fuck him, Mary Ann?" I stared her dead in the eyes to gauge her reaction.

"Wha-wha-what? Are you crazy?" she stuttered, fidgeting in her seat.

"Why does asking the question make me crazy? You did say you liked the way he fucked me. Don't you want him to fuck you like that?"

She lowered her eyes to her knees. "No, I could never do something like that. Isn't he your boyfriend?"

I fell out laughing. "Hell no, I would never let you or anyone else fuck my boyfriend. Drayton is just my piece of dick on the side."

She darted her eyes back up at me. "Piece of dick on the side?"

"Yes. Men do it all the time. They commit themselves in a serious relationship with one woman and then fuck about five or six other ones every chance they get."

She giggled nervously. "That must be a city thing."

"Just admit it," I said, about to issue a challenge. "You're scared shitless."

"Scared of what?"

"Scared of fucking a real man. I bet you're used to two-minute brothas that are only concerned with getting their own nut off instead of pleasing you." I could tell by her expression that I had not only hit the nail on the head but all the way through the fucking head board. "Come on, Mary Ann. Live a little. Drayton would love to rock your world. He's already said as much."

She sat up on the edge of her seat. "What did he say about me?"

"He just asked who you were and why you ran off so quickly after we caught you playing with your little coochie coo. He was hoping we could get a little threesome going."

Fear flashed across her face. "Don't worry, honey. I'm strictly dickly, Mary Ann. We could take turns with Drayton though. That is, if you're woman enough."

Mary Ann bit her bottom lip but refused to respond. I glanced at my watch and realized I had a client due in my office in less than thirty minutes. I tugged at one of Mary Ann's notebooks until she let it go. I opened it and scribbled down an address on a blank piece of paper.

"Meet me at this address tonight at ten," I instructed her. "If you're not there, then so be it."

"Whose address is this?" She stared at the piece of paper.

"Take a wild guess." I winked at her and then got up. I turned to look at her before I let the classroom door close. "Remarkable," was all I had left to say.

11

mary ann

Boy, did I stick my foot in my mouth or what? Or was it more like my entire leg and one of my butt cheeks for good measure! I should have told Olive there was no way on this earth I was meeting her anywhere. But noooo, I had to "go there" as Patricia would put it. Telling Olive she had no sex skills when I didn't have any my damn self.

I left class that afternoon and *literally* barricaded myself in my room. I pushed my bed and my dresser up against the door, then crawled up in the fetal position in a corner and drew the blinds. My knees were shaking, my hands were trembling, and my eyes had this uncontrollable blinking action going on.

About 8 P.M., I was sick of hiding out. My stomach was growling something terrible as well. It sounded like a freight train was barreling through the dorm. I unblocked the door and walked across the street to a deli; dinner service in the cafeteria ended at seven. I got a honey turkey club on rye and found a quiet table in the rear.

Two couples came in a few minutes later. I noticed how lovey-dovey they were and it made me wonder if Trevor and I would ever be like that. Trevor didn't believe in showing affection in public. His reasons probably had much to do with having been intimate with half the women in our campus community. The more I thought about it, the angrier I got. If Trevor could do whatever he wished, if men in general can do whatever they wish, then why can't women?

Something came over me. I was about to do the craziest thing imaginable, at least in my mind. I suddenly felt daring. I wanted to find out what it would be like to be freaky, if only for one night.

I dug through my purse for the address Olive had given me. My fingers were trembling so badly when I pulled the slip of paper out that I dropped it on the floor. As I reached down to get it, I heard someone say, "Here alone?"

I glanced up and saw an older man standing about a foot from my table.

"Yes, I'm here alone."

While not an expert at pick-up lines, I didn't think his was one commonly used in diners. A lot of people eat alone but rarely go to clubs solo.

"Mind if I sit down?" he asked.

"Actually, I'm about to leave," I responded quickly. After taking a better look at him and catching a good whiff of his body odor, I decided that I would never fuck a man like him. Not even for bone marrow.

I got up from the table and headed toward the trash can with my tray of leftovers so I could dump it all.

"Well, maybe some other time," I heard him call after me.

On my way out the door, I got a second wind and a determination to follow through and make that night count for something special. I was trying to flag down a taxi and it occurred to me that I didn't have any condoms. Though I was willing to try freaky sex, I wasn't about to have unsafe sex, and I couldn't rely on Olive and her "piece of dick" having them. I dashed across the street to the drugstore and picked up a three-pack. A taxi was miraculously turning the corner just as I exited the store.

Twenty minutes later, the car pulled up in front of an apartment building in Northwest D.C. I cautiously made my way down the hallway and rapped lightly on the correct door. It swung open within seconds.

There stood sexy-ass Drayton grinning at me. "Looking for Cynda?"

"Who?"

"Cynda."

"Oh yeah, Cynda," I said, remembering that was the name he had called her down that alleyway.

"Come on in," he said, moving aside.

I entered and was surprised to see that his place was so basic. There was a cheap-looking sofa in the middle of the floor and an old, well-worn metal dinette set. The walls were bare except for a Bob Marley poster and a large, felt wall hanging of a marijuana leaf.

It was no surprise then that he soon produced a blunt, or rather the shell of a cigar and packed it with marijuana. He lit it up and asked, "Want to smoke up?"

"Uh, no, thanks." I noticed a door open down the small hallway. "Is Oli—I mean Cynda back there?"

"Yeah, she's here." He took a long hit of the weed and exhaled. "She's taking a quick shower. I like my pussy clean."

"Oh," I said nervously. "Is that right?"

"Damn right! Is your pussy clean?"

I was insulted. His comments were so demeaning and, at the same time, he was turning me on big time. "Why would the hygienic state of my pussy concern you?"

He laughed. "Don't play silly games. We both know why you're here."

"So tell me. Why am I here?"

"Because Cynda hooked it up." He came closer to me and exhaled smoke in my face. "She said you *loved* the way I blew her back out."

"*Loved* is a strong word," I lashed out at him. "But I did find it interesting."

He chortled and took a step back. "Where's your man? I'm sure a fine piece of ass like you has men beating down the door."

"My man is minding his business. Why don't you follow suit and mind yours?"

"Ooh, you're feisty. I like that."

Drayton went over to a small stereo system and threw a twelve-inch on his turntable. I didn't recognize the song but it was some serious reggae. He started gyrating his hips to the music and I couldn't help but stare as he put on a seductive striptease dance for me. He pulled off his white tee and there were muscles rippling for days. Then he kicked off his shoes to reveal bare feet that looked as smooth as silk; just like the rest of him. Next came his pants. He wore no underwear. His dick was *gigantic*. I didn't remember it being quite that big. I tried to hold in the "Damn" that escaped my lips.

Drayton plopped down on his rinky-dink sofa and announced, "It's your turn!"

"My turn?" I sat back in my seat. "Where's Cynda?" I had no intention of stripping in front of a stranger. I had never done that for Trevor or even Clarence when I was still back home. "What's taking her so long?" I asked, attempting to change the subject.

"Cynda will be out here when she gets out here. Now take it all off, baby."

"I would really rather wait for Cynda to come out here."

"Why's that? You want her to freak all over you too?"

"No, nothing like that," I replied, trying to buy some time. "I'd just feel more comfortable with her in here."

He snickered. "Yeah, right."

He got up from the sofa and came toward me. I shuddered for a few seconds when he touched my shoulder. Then his hand dropped to my breast and he started rubbing my nipple through my blouse.

"Don't be nervous, baby." He winked at me and licked his lips. "By the way, what's your name?"

Since Olive was using a fake name for whatever reason, I decided it would be best for me to follow suit. I was drawing a blank though, so I used a line from one of the hooker movies I'd seen on television. "What do you want my name to be?"

He took a deep breath. "Okay, whatever. Your name doesn't matter. I just hope you're not here to play silly games."

Suddenly, I felt revitalized with purpose. Drayton was right. I had showed up at his place on a dare, even though I doubt he knew that. There he was buck naked, ready to "blow my back out" and I was acting like a virgin schoolgirl. It was time for me to either put up or shut up.

I knocked his hand from my breast. "I'm not here to play games."

I unbuttoned my blouse and slipped it off, letting it dangle from my waist. I slid the zipper down in the front of my bra and exposed my breasts. He seemed pleased because he grinned and returned to his sofa so he could seemingly admire the view.

"Are these what you wanted to see?" I asked.

"Those are a good start. Now let's see the rest of you."

I knelt down to untie my boots and then kicked them off one at a time. Then I finished taking my blouse off and slid out of my leggings. The only thing I had left on were a pair of white cotton panties.

"You're a fine bitch!" Drayton said.

"Hey, you can say just about anything to me but never call me a bitch again!" I stated with disdain. He was sexy with a big-ass dick but no man was going to call me a bitch.

He rolled his eyes. "Sorry, baby. That turns some sisters on."

"Well, not this one."

Drayton spread his legs and his hard dick stood up between them like a missile. "Come over here and meet my friend."

"He doesn't look too friendly. In fact, he looks like he can do some serious damage."

"Ahh, I promise he'll be gentle," Drayton said mockingly. "You're not scared of him, are you?"

The fact of the matter was that I was scared shitless but I also wanted to know what he would feel like inside of me. Trevor popped into my head for a moment and I felt a twinge of guilt.

Drayton sighed impatiently and glanced at his bedroom door. "Are we going to do this or not?"

His gesture toward the door made me remember Olive. I had forgotten she was there. I was determined to go through with it, if for no other reason than to keep her from having something to throw in my face. Then again, fucking Drayton would also give her something to throw in my face. I just hoped she never told Patricia. Whatever would she think of me?

I went over and sat beside him on the couch. He leaned over and slid his tongue into my mouth. His kiss was aggressive, something I wasn't quite used to. Everything about him was aggressive. Before I knew it, he had my panties off, had himself situated in between my legs with my heels facing the ceiling, and he was entering me inch by inch.

I pushed him away. "No, you have to wear a condom."

He grinned, got up off the couch and walked over to his entertainment center. He reached behind a speaker and pulled out a little black box. After snapping it open, he removed a condom, ripped the packet open with his teeth and eased it on his dick.

After coming back to the couch, Drayton palmed one of my breasts and sucked on my nipple to divert my attention from the fact that he was stretching my pussy to its limit. I moaned, half in ecstasy and half in pain. What in the hell had I gotten myself into?

olive

That little slut! Trying to put up a front like she was so timid. I peeked out the bedroom door and saw Drayton fucking the hell out of the country bumpkin. Even though Drayton was just a piece of dick to me, I still wasn't too thrilled about sharing it; especially with her. But it was kind of interesting. After all, she did actually have the nerve to show up. Maybe Patricia was onto something after all.

I had listened to their conversation from the second Mary Ann had come into the apartment. I didn't want to go out there because I figured she would chicken out or something. I never expected her to come, much less strip down to her drawers and let him tap that ass.

I had the shower on, as a cover, and the steam was emitting from the bathroom door into the bedroom. The heat from the shower and watching them get it on made me kind of horny. It was almost like one of our APF freak nights except I wasn't getting busy myself.

Drayton pulled out after about ten minutes and flipped Mary Ann over so he could tap that ass doggy-style. My personal favorite when it comes to positions. Mary Ann dug her nails into the armrest of the sofa, like she was holding on for dear life. She had obviously been fucked before but it was also obvious that Drayton was laying something on her she had never experienced—the good dick. I couldn't take it anymore. I needed to get off. I laid down on the bed, reached into my purse and pulled out Jiggy, my silver-plated vibrator, slid my red satin panties to the side, placed him on my clit, and got jiggy with myself until I came.

After I was done, I got back up and went to the door to see what the two of them were doing. Good thing I did because Drayton was saying that he wanted to taste her. Oh, no. That shit was not about to happen. I swung the door open and walked over to the couch.

"Um, I think that's enough," I said nastily.

They both looked up at me. Drayton had this big grin on his face and Mary Ann's eyes were glazed over. She took a deep breath, like she had forgotten I was there.

"Did you have fun, *freak?*" I asked her.

She knocked Drayton off her, got up and started scrambling for her clothes.

"Answer me, *freak*. Did you have fun?"

Drayton grabbed my wrist. "Ease up, Cynda. You're the one that set this up. Don't tell me you're jealous."

"That would make your fucking day, wouldn't it?" I asked him, pulling my wrist away. "Sorry, but I'm not jealous. Just bored."

Drayton stood up on his knees on the couch, and pulled me by the waist toward him as I leaned over the back of the couch. He sucked on my neck. "I have something for your boredom. You know you're still my number one."

Hmph, I thought. He damn sure wasn't my number one. "Drayton, I'm about to go."

He moved his head down to my breasts and started biting them gently in turn. "You can't go. You and I have business to take care of."

"Looks like you already handled your business for tonight," I said, glaring at Mary Ann who looked like a kid with her hand caught in a cookie jar.

Drayton laughed. "See, you are jealous."

Mary Ann didn't say a word. She dressed and exited out the door. I started to go after her but decided against it. On one hand, I couldn't believe she'd fucked him. On the other hand, I was proud as hell of her for letting go of whatever inhibitions she might have had before she showed up.

"Remarkable," I whispered aloud.

"Yes, we are remarkable together," Drayton whispered back as he tried to get my panties lowered.

I smirked at him. "You talk so much shit. Shut up and eat my pussy."

"Serve it up!"

12

patricia

"Mary Ann, why are you avoiding me?" It took me almost three hours to track the ole girl down. I finally found her lurking in the stacks at the law library.

She gazed up at me, trying to look naive and innocent. "What do you mean?"

"Oh, come off it, don't play with me."

"I'm serious." She took off her eyeglasses, which up to that point I didn't even know she wore, and placed them on the oak table beside a pile of books. "What are you talking about?"

I sat down across the table from her and stared her ass down. "I'm talking about the fact that I hardly ever see you anymore."

"That's because I've been spending a lot of time over Trevor's." I rolled my eyes. *They were really taking the shit a little too far.* "He's asked me to move in with him next semester."

"You've got to be shittin' me!" I forgot all about being in the library. A couple of students sitting at another table started glaring at us. I threw them an evil leer.

"No, he really did," Mary Ann whispered.

"This is asinine." I couldn't hold in my opinion a second longer. "You need to dump his ass with a quickness and find a *real* man."

"Trevor is a *real* man and he's very good to me."

I rolled my eyes again and smacked my lips for added effect. "Your life. Your mistakes. Your drama."

"Maybe you should just go." She picked her glasses back up and put them on. "I have tons of studying to do. I've been falling behind lately."

"Okay, whatever." I got up from the table. "I was just trying to be your friend."

"I know and I appreciate everything you and Olive have done for me."

"Olive?" I was stunned. "What the hell has Olive ever done for you? You only met her that one time and, even then, she came off extremely nasty toward you."

"You're right," Mary Ann uttered. "I have no idea why I even said that." She glanced at her watch and then started gathering her books. "I really have to go. I have class in fifteen minutes." I knew her ass was lying. Two seconds earlier, she was insisting that I leave so she could study. "We'll hang out soon. I promise."

I watched her half walk, half run away. I didn't know what

the fuck was going on between her and Olive but I was damn sure going to find out.

I barged into Olive's waiting room and demanded to see her right away. One of her administrative assistants said she was in with a patient and had two others waiting in examination rooms. I insisted on waiting and she told me I could wait in Olive's private office.

It took her a good hour to finish up, but I wasn't about to budge. "Whew, these chicas are getting on my last nerve!" she blared, coming into her office and slamming the door behind her.

"What chicas?" I was sitting in one of the visitor wing chairs in front of her desk, flipping through an issue of *Fitness* magazine.

She plopped down in her black leather desk chair and threw her feet on the desktop. "My patients. The holidays are coming up and all of them want to look like they're twenty-one again."

I chuckled. "Well, that means more money for you, right?"

"Damn right it does!" She took her feet back down and squirmed in her chair, trying to find a comfortable position. "I don't mean to be rude, sissypoo, but I'm swamped today. What brings you by my office? This is a first."

I opted to get straight to the point. "The strangest thing happened earlier today."

We sat there staring at each other for a few seconds. "Well, are you going to tell me sometime today, or do I have to guess?" Olive asked sarcastically.

"I saw Mary Ann over in the library and she mentioned you."

"And?" Olive raised her brow. She folded her hands across her chest and proceeded to play with her collar. That's when I knew she was up to something. Olive always meddles with her collar when she's lying. I don't even think she realizes it.

"She said that she appreciated everything you've done for her." I looked at her accusingly, letting her know I was up on the game.

"Is that right?" She sat there, still messing with that damn shirt collar.

"Uh-huh. My question is, what the hell did you do?"

"My next patient will be here any second," she blurted out, standing back up and getting a manila folder out of the in box on her credenza. "Maybe we can meet up later for a cup of java."

"Fugg a java!" I was pissed off and I wanted her to know it. "What did you do to Mary Ann?"

"I didn't do a damn thing to her," she stated defensively. "I just—"

"Just what?"

"Aiight, damn!" There she went. Her ghetto side reared its ugly head and I knew we were about to have it out. "I caught Miss Hee Haw doing a Peeping Tom act on Drayton and me down an alley in Adams Morgan."

I catapulted out of my seat. "Get the fuck out of here!"

"I kid you not. Not only was she spying, she was getting her freak on in the process." Olive giggled and sat back down in her desk chair. She gave me a wicked look and added, "We caught her fingering herself behind a wall."

"Get the fuck out of here!" I repeated, sitting down on the edge of her desk less than two feet away from her.

"I was furious, to say the least. You know how I get? Especially when I'm trying to relieve PID symptoms."

"Yeah, I know how you get," I replied. The sorors and I tried to steer clear of Olive when she was suffering through PID. It was truly a bitch!

"I mean, I have no problem fucking in front of other people at freak nights and shit, but Drayton's always been my private dick supply."

I prodded her to continue with the story. "So what happened after you caught her?"

"She ran away." We both fell out laughing.

I shook my head in disbelief. "I have a feeling it didn't end there."

"Hellz naw, it didn't! I tracked her down in class the very next day and told her ass off."

I could imagine how Olive must've laid into Mary Ann. I instantly felt sorry for her. "She must've felt so ashamed."

"She was practically begging me not to mention it to you." Olive tossed the folder on her desk and sucked in her bottom lip. "But then she had the nerve to break bad with my ass."

"Mary Ann?" I tried to picture Mary Ann breaking bad with anyone. Although she did get pretty irritated with Olive the first time they met.

"Yeah, gurl, she went there."

"What did she say?"

"She tried to play me for a fool, saying she wasn't impressed with my skillz at all and that she could do better." Olive chuckled. "Imagine that!"

"Word?" I couldn't help but laugh. Olive swore up and down she had the bomb-ass pussy so I knew she was highly offended when Mary Ann came off at her like that. She was just trying to fake the funk about it. "So then what happened?"

"I called her mutha fuckin' bluff! What do you think I did?"

"No, you didn't?" I asked, wondering what calling her bluff entailed exactly.

"Wanna bet?" Olive took a tube of lipstick out of her purse and applied it perfectly without the benefit of a mirror. "I told her to meet me at Drayton's apartment later that night."

I almost fainted at the prospect. "Surely she didn't show?"

"I had just come to the conclusion that she was all talk and no action when she knocked on the door. I hid in the back, pretending to take a shower, until he'd busted her wide open."

"She fucked him?"

Olive smirked. "I wouldn't say all that but he fucked the living daylights out of her."

"This is too much!" I couldn't even believe the shit was going down like that. I thought Mary Ann was strung out over Trevor.

"Isn't it though?" Olive asked rhetorically. "I'll have to admit that the chica has chutzpah. She might just be APF material after all."

"This is unfuckenbelievable!" I got up from the desk and started pacing the floor. "All this time I've been trying to think of a tactful way to break her sexual barrier and you had her up in Drayton's crib fuckin' and shit." Before Olive could respond, her administrative assistant's voice blared out over the intercom on her desk. "Mrs. Wallingford's here for her tummy tuck."

Olive hissed and smacked her lips. "Listen up, my next appointment is here." She got up from her chair and threw the lipstick back in her purse. "We'll chat later."

"How about we meet up for that cup of java at Starbucks a little later?" My curiosity had been piqued. I wanted to know every little detail of what went on in Drayton's apartment.

"I can be there by six." Olive opened her office door and walked out into the hallway.

"Cool." I followed suit. "Then we can discuss what our next move will be with Mary Ann."

13

mary ann

Talk about a rough day! It wasn't so much rough as it was traumatic. First, I go check my mailbox in the lobby of the dorm and I find this slip telling me that I had an oversized package, too large for my box. The work-study student behind the front desk handed it to me. It was from Clarence.

He is so childish! He had the audacity to send me belongings that I'd left behind at his place, including my pink cotton underwear set, an old pair of my reading glasses, a gray wool sweater,and a pair of socks. Yes, I said socks. What type of trifling man would send such things cross-country? I'll tell you what type. The same type that would try to turn his infidelities around on me. *Infidelity* is a harsh word, especially since I was dating Trevor, sleeping with Trevor, and had indulged in that freaky behavior with Drayton.

But, Clarence still had a lot of damn nerve. I was ready to move forward. In fact, that same day I was planning to tell Trevor I'd move in with him the next semester. We were spending a lot of time together. We had engaged in sex quite a bit and that had gotten better as we became more comfortable with one another. He still couldn't touch my experience with Drayton though. I can't rightly say I was in love with Trevor at that point, but the feelings were strong. I guess that's why what happened later that afternoon hurt so much. It cut right down to the bone.

I caught a cab over to Trevor's town house to tell him the news of my decision to live with him. I was all the more excited after getting Clarence's bullshit package. My elation didn't last long. It faded like a certain pop star's skin. I rang the doorbell, expecting my man to open it.

Instead, FeFe did. "Come on in," she said, like she was the woman of the house.

I knocked her ass out of my way. I stepped into the foyer, yelled out, "Trevor! Trevor!" I kept shouting as I went from the living room, to the kitchen, and then up the steps.

"He's not here." FeFe looked as snug as a bug in a rug. "He went to the store."

"His car's outside. Stop lying," I hissed back at her.

"Trevor took my car." She grinned. "He just loves the way I ride, I mean the way my car rides."

"Well, bitch, I ride him better."

She slammed the front door and folded her arms, trying to take a threatening stance. "You're just some fly-by-night pussy for Trevor. He'll come back to me. He knows where the good pussy lives."

"Is that right?" I asked.

"This little thing between you and Trevor has gone far enough. He and I have been fucking since our sophomore year of undergrad. It's time he made a commitment to me."

I fell out laughing. "Well, I think you better notify him of all that because he told me he plans to settle down with me."

Her face turned as pale as a ghost. "He would never do that to me."

"Huh! The reason I'm here today is to tell Trevor that I'm moving in," I boasted.

"Moving in?" She balled her hands into fists and let them hang at her sides. "Over my dead body."

"You don't have much of a body."

"That might be, but I have one hell of a mouth." She flicked her tongue out at me. "Just ask Trevor. He tastes so good, doesn't he?"

FeFe was damn lucky I wasn't prone to violence because that is the only thing that stood between her and the ass-kicking of a lifetime. "Whatever happened between you and Trevor in the past is irrelevant."

"The past?" She cackled. "You mean the past thirty minutes?"

"Stop trying to run a game on me! I know you're lying! Trevor didn't fuck you!"

"Not technically. He just fucked my mouth."

I was about to throw all of my home-training out the window and beat her beanpole anorexic ass. Then I heard Trevor's key in the lock. He came in, wiping his feet on the welcome mat, carrying a paper grocery bag. "FeFe, I'm back! How about another round?"

"Trevor, your slut of the month is here," FeFe announced.

He looked up, spotted me, and dropped the bag. Something glass inside of it shattered and liquid started seeping through onto the floor. "Mary Ann, I can explain this. I don't know what she told you, but I really can explain."

"You know what, Trevor? Keep your fucking explanation!"

I stormed past him and out of the house, walking down the street having no clue where I was going. I remembered seeing a Metro bus stop a couple of blocks over so I headed in that direction. I found the stop and was sitting on the bench fuming when Trevor pulled up in his Porsche.

"Get in the car, Mary Ann," he demanded.

"For what?" I smacked my lips. "Isn't *Miss Hoover* still waiting for you at your place?" He cut his engine and got out of the car. "You're wasting your time if you seriously think I'm going anywhere with you. The only place I'm going is back to campus."

"The bus that comes through here doesn't even go that way," he stated, as if that would make me get into his car.

"Well, I'll go wherever then." He sat down beside me on the bench and reached for me. "Don't fucking touch me!" I knocked his hand away. "Don't *ever* fucking touch me!"

"You're being ridiculous," he remarked. "FeFe means nothing to me. I already told you what I need in my life and where I want this thing between you and me to go."

"Yes, you did tell me your pack of lies." I rolled my eyes in his direction. "I even believed your crock of bullshit and was all prepared to take you up on your offer of living together."

"Really?" he squealed, blushing. For what, I don't know, because I hated his ass right then.

"I caught a cab over here so we could finalize some plans, maybe make love afterward, but *noooo*. You're too busy getting your dick sucked to be thinking about me."

Trevor reached for me again and I scooted down farther on the bench. "Mary Ann, we just need to go back to my place and dis—"

"What about your bitch?"

"She's gone and she's not coming back!"

"Yeah, right!"

"I'm serious," he pleaded. "You're my heart!"

"Are you denying that she gave you a blow job today?" I glared at him so I could tell if he was full of it when he answered.

Trevor diverted his eyes to the ground. "It was a mistake. I was stressed out over one of my classes and she's in the same class. She told me she'd help me study so I let her come over and—"

"Let me guess! One thing led to another? Somehow your pants ended up around your ankles and your dick ended up in her mouth?"

"That sounds so crude."

"Crude or not, she sucked your dick and that's the bottom line." I took a deep, restorative breath. "You might think I'm stupid since I grew up on a farm, but nothing could be further from the truth."

"I don't think that at all, baby," he insisted. "Come on. Let's just go before I get a ticket for parking in a bus zone."

"Speaking of buses," I said, spotting a Metro bus turning the corner. "My ride's here."

"Mary Ann, stop being silly!" Trevor blared angrily. "You're coming with me! You're not getting on a damn bus!"

I stood up and dug through my purse for some change. "Watch me!" The bus pulled up behind Trevor's car and started blowing its horn because he was illegally parked. I hopped on the bus as soon as the doors swung open. Trevor tried to grab my elbow, but I paid my fare, rushed to the back of the bus, and took a seat.

The bus driver told him to get off the bus if he wasn't riding. He searched through his pockets and realized he didn't have any change. "Mary Ann, get off the bus, dammit!"

"Kiss my ass!" The other riders stared at the interchange between the two of us. "For the last time, it's over, Trevor!"

Trevor sulked back down the bus steps, having run out of options. The driver closed the doors and took off. I peered out the back window and saw Trevor kicking his tires and yelling expletives.

Once we'd gone about a mile, I realized I had no idea where I was going. I asked an older Hispanic woman sitting beside me, "Where does this bus go?"

"Adams Morgan," she replied.

"Adams Morgan," I whispered to myself, suddenly coming to two conclusions. One, Drayton lived in Adams Morgan, and two, payback is a bitch.

I had no trouble finding Drayton's apartment building. The last stop was directly across the street from it. For a brief moment I was leery of going in there. What if Olive was there with him? What if someone else was? What if Olive found out I had come back there? Would she be mad?

Finally I said, fuck it! Olive was the one that introduced me to his sex in the first place. She couldn't justify being angry with me for making a return visit. Besides, for all I knew, he might not even be home. I decided to chance it.

I passed a couple of suspicious-looking characters in the hallway and proceeded to bang on Drayton's door without the slightest hesitation. It was almost as if I could smell his dick. I was so furious at Trevor that I was down for just about anything.

Drayton swung the door open so fast that it made me jump back a couple of steps. "Well, well." He licked his lips and looked me up and down. "To what do I owe this surprise?" He poked his head out of the door and looked down the hallway. "Where's Cynda?"

"She didn't come with me," I blurted out, almost forgetting about Olive's pseudonym. "Is that a problem?"

"It's not a problem for me if it's not a problem for you." He chuckled and moved aside. "Come on in, my little country princess."

"Stop making reference to my upbringing," I replied, going inside and sitting down on his couch. "I hate it when people tease me about my accent. People fail to realize that before I came to D.C., everyone around me sounded exactly like me. So it's not my fault."

He pressed his palms down toward the floor. "Calm down, baby! I was only joking."

"Okay, cool." I took off my wool blazer and laid it over the armrest. "I didn't come here to talk anyway."

"Oh really?" Drayton sat down on the coffee table and spread my legs open with his own, exposing the white cotton panties I was wearing under a plaid skirt, a white blouse, and knee-length socks. "What did you come here for, then?" I hesitated. He arched a brow and repeated the question. "What did you come for?"

Tell him the damn truth, I said to myself. "I came for the dick."

He threw his head back in laughter, his long dreads covering his shoulder blades. "I like a blunt woman."

"And I like a big-dick man."

"It's on," he whispered and then pounced on me like a bear to a pot of honey. We started tonguing the hell out of each other. I went for his zipper in a matter of seconds. He came up for air. "Damn, you're not fucking around, are you, baby? You mean business."

I struggled to catch my breath, finding the zipper and yanking it down. "Like I said, I didn't come here to talk."

"In that case, let me give you something else to do with that pretty-ass mouth of yours." He stood up, dropped his pants to the floor, and straddled me on the couch with his knees, knocking me in the forehead with his gigantic dick. "You didn't want to taste me last time, remember? How about today? You up for this?" I pondered his question. I'd never sucked Trevor's dick; not once. I'd done Clarence a few times, or at least tried to, but he seemed so nervous and came so quick that I decided it wasn't even worth the effort. Drayton's dick looked twice as huge as it did last time and only one word came to mind. *Choke!*

"I can try it, but I'm not very good at this," I answered.

"It's okay. I'm a very patient man, baby. Take your time and savor the moment."

I took a deep breath and then slid the head of it into my mouth and thought, Oh damn! Just the tip of it was damn near hitting the back of my throat. I tried to fit a little bit more of it in and immediately started gagging.

He pulled it out of my mouth. "Hold up, let's try this another way." He climbed off the couch and then sat down beside me. "Just lick it at first and then do a little more once you feel more comfortable."

I got down on my knees between his legs and started licking the shaft like it was a gigantic ice cream cone. A ten scoop one. Shit, maybe twelve. He reached for his remote control and turned off his television. "I want to hear you do me. I love the way it sounds."

I placed small kisses all over him and then gathered his ball sack in my palm and kissed that as well. He started moaning and so did I. I had flashbacks of all the porn films I watched back in South Dakota and tried to remember the different techniques I'd witnessed.

After about ten minutes of kissing and licking his dick, I felt it was time to go a little further. I took the head back in and this time I was able to relax the back of my throat so I didn't gag. I started moving my warm mouth up and down on it and he moaned louder. I darted my eyes up at him because I wanted to see the expression on his face. I wanted to see if he looked like the guys from the movies. Like he was in a state of bliss. He had that *look* and that inspired me to go for the gusto.

I took as much of it in as I could possibly handle, about half, and then started taking it in and out faster and rubbing my hand up and down the remainder and caressing his balls. "Damn, baby!" he screamed out in pleasure. "That's what I'm talking about!"

My cheeks began to get sore and I had to take a breather. I had every intention of continuing, but Drayton obviously had other plans. "Get up," he instructed. I did and then he took me by the hand into his bedroom. He began to get undressed. I followed suit until we were both naked. He took two pillows and placed them on top of each other in the center of his bed and then laid me down on the bed with my stomach on the pillows. "I've been having this wild fantasy about you since the last time you were here. I wish I'd done this last time but you ran out so fast."

"I was scared," I admitted, trying to position my hands so I would be comfortable. I had the feeling I was in for a coochie beating for real—the way he was rubbing my ass like he was priming it for serious action.

"Are you scared now?"

"No!" I exclaimed. "I want to experience new things."

"That's good because you're about to experience something awesome."

I squealed when he entered me suddenly and tried to relax. I'd almost forgotten how far Drayton's dick went inside me. It was even deeper this time because of the positioning. He grabbed onto my ass cheeks, one in each hand, and then proceeded to fuck the living daylights out of me. I started moaning so loud and making such strange noises that I found it hard to believe it was even me making them. I dug my nails into the mattress and hung on for dear life.

He fucked me royally and then pulled it out just in time to cum all over my backside. I lay there trying to breathe. Sweat was trickling down my forehead onto the pillows.

We fell asleep in that position for a couple of hours until the phone blared out and woke us up. Drayton climbed off me and grabbed the cordless off his nightstand. "Hello," he gasped into the phone. There was a brief pause and then he said, "Oh hello, *Cynda*," stressing her name.

I leapt off the bed and started grabbing my clothes. He giggled and grabbed me by the wrists, shaking his head. "Hold on for a second." He placed the phone up to his shoulder blade, covering the mouthpiece. "You're not going to get away from me so fast this time."

I sat back down and pulled a sheet up over my body, feeling guilty about being there without Olive's permission.

"Cynda, can you hit me back some other time?" he asked. There was another brief pause and then he hung up the phone without even saying goodbye. "It's all cool now. She won't be calling back tonight." He sat down beside me. "Want to take a shower? I could eat you out."

I considered his proposition. He did have a way with that tongue of his and I figured his oral sex had to be the ultimate, but then my mind wandered to Trevor. How could I blame him for doing something I was so easily capable of? To the best of my knowledge, I'd cheated on him before he even cheated on me with FeFe. But I wasn't sure I ever wanted to lay eyes on Trevor again. I wasn't sure about anything.

"Thanks for the offer, but I really have to go." Drayton sighed and pressed his dreads back away from his face with his palms. "I had a great time though," I added.

"Will I ever see you again?" He held my hand and I started trembling. "Are you cold?"

"No, I'm fine," I lied. "I just need to get back to campus because I have a lot of studying to do."

"What school do you go to?"

That's when I realized Drayton didn't know a damn thing about me. I quickly discerned that it was better to keep it that way so I lied again. "I go to UDC."

"That's cool. What are you studying?"

"Premed," I replied.

"Aw, a doctor." He chuckled. "I suppose you do have tons of work to do then."

"Yes, I really do." I started to get dressed. After I was done, he walked me to the door. I looked him in the eyes. "Can you do me a huge favor, Drayton?"

"What's that?"

"Could you not mention my visit to Cynda?"

He laughed and sucked his teeth. "Cynda and I aren't married. What happens between the two of us is our business." He lifted my hand and sucked my index finger. "I just hope you cum—I mean come again."

I blushed and opened the door, stepping out into the hallway. I wasn't quite sure what to say so I just said, "Take care."

"You too," he replied, waving at me while I walked down the hall backward.

I returned to the dorm and locked myself in, ashamed and confused. Patricia knocked on my door a couple of times but I didn't answer. There was no way she could tell whether I was there or not. I was lying on the bed in the dark with nothing on. I heard her holding a casual conversation with a couple of other female students in the hall and then I heard her door slam. While I had mixed feelings about Trevor, Drayton, and life in general, one thing was for sure. I was changing and sex had become more than just something to do to please a man. It had become all about pleasing me. I could only view that as a good thing. I fell asleep with a smile on my face.

14

patricia

I was on my way out of class one Friday after-noon when I spotted Yvette headed my way. She had that *look*. It was obvious she was frustrated and part of me wanted to avoid her ass and head in the other direction. Before I could decide what to do, she yelled out to me.

"Patricia, hold up!"

"Shit, too late," I mumbled to myself before throwing a fake smile on my face. "Hey, Yvette. What's up, girl?"

"Just got out of class! I hate that fucking professor!"

"Which professor?" I asked, even though I couldn't have cared less.

"Professor Hall."

"Oh, that bitch!" Professor Hall was the queen bitch on campus and tried to fail people right and left. She really had it in for the sisters that were trying to make it in the law profession. She was an older white woman and I had the distinct feeling that she wanted us to stay in "our place."

"Yeah, I am sick to death of her," Yvette said, rubbing her forehead like she was battling a migraine. "So, what are you doing tonight?"

"Not a damn thing. I was just planning to get a jump start on a term paper and maybe check out a movie."

"Hmph, sounds boring as shit!"

We both laughed as we walked side by side toward the student union. It was almost dinnertime and my stomach was growling something fierce.

"When is freak night?"

"Same time it always is, Yvette. The last Saturday of the month."

She shook her head. "I don't know if I can make it that long."

My nosy side automatically raised its ugly head. "You're not banging someone on the regular?"

"Naw, you?"

"No. I was but his job transferred him."

"Too bad."

"Way too bad. The brother was hung like a horse."

We both fell out laughing again.

Yvette stopped in her tracks. "Listen, it's been a long time since we've been out trolling together."

I grinned at her, running the memories of our wild times through my head. "It has been a minute."

"A minute? It's been more like an hour." Yvette nudged me. "So how about it? It'll be just like the good old days."

"Where are we going to go?" I asked.

"Who cares? Does it really matter?"

I shrugged. "I guess not."

"Cool, so what time do you want to roll out?"

"Tonight?"

"Yeah, tonight," Yvette replied. "Why put it off? I need some action and I need it now."

"Girl, you're off the chain," I told her before glancing at my watch. "It's going on four now so let's meet up about eight in my dorm room."

"Sounds like a winner. See you then."

After dinner, I caught a couple hours of sleep before I got dressed for a night of trolling. Trolling for sex was something Yvette and I started doing our first year in law school, after we both ended up as members of APF. Freak nights are the bomb but sometimes we wanted to venture out on our own.

I squeezed my ass into this skintight black catsuit and slid into some four-inch spike heels. I looked like a whore but that was exactly the look I was going for. Undoubtedly, Yvette would show up in something just as raunchy. We were on a mission to get our freak on and nothing else. No strings. No attachments. Just good, old-fashioned fucking.

There was a knock on my door and I assumed it was Yvette. I was stunned to open the door and find Mary Ann on the other side.

"Mary Ann, what's going on?" I asked, stepping aside to let her enter.

"Nothing much." She came in and plopped down on my bed. I noticed that she was wearing makeup and had a fancy hairstyle. Sistergurl was moving up in the world. "I thought you might want to take in a movie or something."

"No hot date with Trevor tonight?" I asked sarcastically.

"Trevor had a family emergency and had to go to Indiana for the weekend."

I had the distinct feeling that she was lying. I had known Trevor for years and he rarely went home, even for school breaks and holidays. He seemed to harbor a deep hatred for his parents or something. "Oh, is everything all right?"

"I guess. He left me a note but it didn't explain much. Just that he had to leave and he would be back on Tuesday."

"I see." I noticed the way she was eyeing my outfit and I really didn't feel like explaining myself so I decided to rush her out of my room. "Well, I would go with you but I have plans. Maybe we can catch a matinee tomorrow."

She got up from the bed and headed toward the door. "I'll look forward to it." She paused in the doorway. "Are you going to a club?"

"I'm not sure. I just told a friend we could hang out tonight."

"Oh. Well, have fun."

I could tell that Mary Ann felt left out and was hoping I would invite her but she wasn't ready for that type of action yet.

"Thanks. I'll come by your room tomorrow and we can check out what's playing. I heard Denzel has a new movie out."

"Um, I just love Denzel," Mary Ann commented. "He's so fine."

"Girl, please. You ain't never lied."

We both giggled.

"See you tomorrow."

"Peace."

I watched Mary Ann traipse across the hall and into her room. No sooner had she closed the door than Yvette came down the hall from the elevator in a skimpy yellow dress that showed just about everything her momma gave her.

"Girl, you're looking hot!" Yvette yelled out.

"You too!" I grabbed my keys and pulled my door shut. I didn't want Mary Ann to peep out of her room and spot us. Not that it would've seemed strange. She already knew that Yvette and I knew each other. For some reason, I just didn't want her to think that I was choosing one over the other. It wasn't even like that. Yvette and I were cool but we were far from best friends. We just had the love of good dick in common.

About an hour later, we pulled up in front of a nightclub in Woodbridge, Virginia. We liked to go a safe distance from the school when we were on a troll. They say there are six degrees of separation in society but with black folks, it is more like two. We didn't want to stand the risk of being found out.

Before we went in, we primped in the car mirrors.

"So who are you tonight?" Yvette asked me.

"Hmm, I think I'll be Blaze tonight."

"I love that name." Yvette threw her eyes up in her head, deep in thought. "I think I'll be Caramel."

"Sweet and nasty, huh?" I teased.

"You know it!"

We slapped each other a high five and went into the club. It was packed from wall to wall, which wasn't saying much since it was a rather small establishment. We had never been there before but we had heard of it through the grapevine. Rumor had it that a lot of fine black bikers frequented the place. Bikers tend to be roughnecks and Yvette and I shared a thing for the type.

We hadn't been there five minutes when the two men we were searching out approached us at the bar and offered to buy us drinks. Both of them seemed to be in their early thirties. One was tall, light-skinned, and bald. He was the one for me. I just love bald-headed men. The other one was shorter but still teetering about six feet, butter pecan, and had a nice little fade and a goatee.

After we were all settled into a booth, the games began.

"So, you sisters from around here?" Baldy asked.

"Actually, we're from West Virginia," I lied. "We decided to hang out in the big city tonight."

The two men looked at each other and laughed. "If you call this a big city, I wonder what you would say about Washington,

D.C.," Baldy said. "Woodbridge is a small community compared to that."

Yvette played dumb and even threw a serious countrified accent into the mix. "Really? I've never been there." She wrapped her arm around the bicep of the shorter one and added, "Maybe you can take me there one day."

"Sure," he said, blushing. "I'll take you anywhere you want to go."

Yvette looked at me and winked. "Does that include to bed?"

Baldy almost choked on his beer while I held in a laugh. His friend looked like he was searching for a response.

Yvette repeated the question. "Does that include to bed?"

Finally, he responded, "Absolutely! If you're serious."

"I never joke about getting my pussy eaten."

Baldy really started choking then. I had to slap him on the back. I started wondering if he would be a lousy lay. After all, if Yvette talking shit was causing him to flip, what would he do when I laid it on him?

His friend threw his hands up in the air. "Hey, I never said anything about eating pussy. I don't even know your name."

"My name's Caramel and I taste just as sweet." Yvette leaned over and sucked on his earlobe. I was tempted to peek under the table because he had to be rock hard.

Baldy looked at me. "What's your name?"

"Blaze."

"Blaze?"

"Yes, I got that nickname from men friends," I lied.

"How come?"

"Because my pussy's hotter than the flames of hell."

Baldy cleared his throat. "Damn, you sisters don't be bull-shitting."

The temptation was just too much so I rubbed his head. "You have a name, stud muffin?"

"My name's Luis."

I looked toward his friend. "And his name is?"

"Michael. Mike for short."

I reached down into his lap and started caressing his dick. "Umm, it feels like you're packing. How many inches are you?"

He gave me one of the craziest looks I had ever seen. "Are you for real?"

I unzipped his pants and maneuvered my hand down into them until I had a firm grip on his dick. "Why don't we go someplace quiet and you can find out whether or not I'm for real?"

"You have somewhere in mind?"

"The closest damn hotel, motel, or shitty-ass place we can find. As long as it has a bed, it's all good."

Yvette moved in closer to Michael. "What about you? You down for this?"

He grinned. "Shit, I'm down for whatever."

Within fifteen minutes, we were walking into a room at a hotel by the Interstate. It was rather nice, so I was kind of disap-pointed. When we were trolling, Yvette and I liked to role-play like we were damn near hookers or something. Most hookers had to give up the ass in dumps, but the place Luis and Michael took us to was rather lavish. It had a kitchen, sofa, and two queen-sized beds. Another disappointment was that they weren't bikers. It turned out that Luis was an accountant and Michael was a real estate agent. Not exactly the things raunchy fantasies are made of. When Michael asked if we'd like him to make some coffee, I almost hurled. A cup of coffee as a prelude to fucking?

Luis had actually offered to take us back to his place, which was a serious no-no. I wasn't even trying to get to know him like that. He asked me what I did for a living and I told him that I raised chickens. I had no idea what people did to make ends meet in West Virginia, so I stole the idea from Mary Ann's background. The look of disbelief on his face told me that he wasn't really buying it but I didn't care. Come sunrise the man would never lay eyes on me again, if I had anything to say about it.

Michael drove a big-ass Blazer. I hoped that didn't mean he had a Napoleon complex. Sometimes men try to surround themselves with big things to make up for the little things they are holding. I knew Yvette and if the brotha was seriously lacking in the dick department, she would have no problem straight up embarrassing him in front of Luis and me. Besides, I was hoping to turn the night into a foursome and I could not stand little dicks either.

Luis and I had made out in the elevator on the way up to the seventh floor. He was a great kisser. That's for damn sure. It had been a while since a man had kissed me with such passion. I wondered if that was normal for him or if he had been going through a pussy drought and was making up for lost time. I definitely didn't want him to get pussy-whipped. However, if he did end up that way, it was a personal problem because I was moving out and moving on.

After checking out the amenities of the room, we cut out all the lights except the one in the bathroom. That left us just enough visibility to see who was who. I flipped through the stations on the digital alarm clock and finally landed on an R & B station that was in the middle of a slow jam marathon.

Yvette and I stood in the middle of the two beds and started dancing seductively together. It was something we had done many times before and it never failed to turn men on. She ran her fingers through my hair while I slid the straps of her dress off her shoulders. When her breasts toppled out, I could have sworn that I heard one of the men gasp. Yvette had nice tits but they weren't humongous. Hell, if she had been holding triple Ds, someone might have fainted.

It took another ten minutes or so for us to completely undress each other. We took our time and did it slowly so the men could take in every inch one at a time. Luis was laid back on one of the beds while Michael was sitting on the edge of the other one.

I sat on the octagonal table and leaned back on my elbows, spreading my legs. I eyed Luis seductively. "Anyone care for a snack?"

Luis was frozen and it tripped me out when Michael jumped up from the bed and sat down between my legs within a matter of seconds. He didn't say a word. He just started getting his grub on. That was surprising considering his reaction to Yvette's pussy-eating comment back at the club.

I knew Yvette wouldn't care about the sudden partner

switcheroo. Luis was hands down the finer of the two. I would have bitched about it if the tongue action hadn't been on point. Michael went tongue-diving for a good fifteen minutes while I watched Yvette climb on top of Luis on the bed and start kissing him. She pulled his shirt over his head and then bit at his nipples. Most women don't understand that men tend to get more stimulated by nipple play than women.

Yvette helped Luis get his pants off and started waxing his dick. I always told Yvette that if she ever flunked out of law school, she could definitely star in pornos. I knew how to suck a mean dick but Yvette had that shit down to a science. What amazes me about her is that even if a man is humongous, Yvette can take the whole thing in her mouth like it's a lollipop.

Quite frankly, watching her suck Luis's dick started to turn me on more than Michael eating my pussy. Everything is okay in moderation but I was ready for some fucking. I pushed Michael's face away from me and said, "Get naked and sit over there on the sofa."

He obeyed and I got a condom out of my purse. I was glad to see that Michael was well endowed. I sat down beside him and kissed him so I could taste my own pussy. I just love the way I taste. When I was back in high school, I used to lie in the bed, finger myself, and lick my fingers. Some people might find that nasty but if a woman doesn't want to taste herself, then why should a man?

I glanced over at the bed and Luis and Yvette were doing each other orally. Now that's what I was talking about. The "69" position has always been a personal favorite. While I enjoyed seeing them go at it, I was ready to sit on some good old-fashioned dick. I mounted Michael like he was a stallion and eased his dick inside my pussy.

"Um," I said to him. "You feel damn good, baby!"

He palmed my breasts and started lapping on my left nipple like an ice-cream cone. "You feel good too, sweetie!"

I turned around and winked at Yvette, who was about to slap a condom on Luis. Then she and I made a game of it; trying to see who could ride a dick the best. It was something we often did when we went trolling. So many women are scared to ride dicks. They think there's something difficult about it, but it's really all a matter of attitude and self-confidence.

Not only did Yvette and I fuck the two brothas hard, we fucked them right to sleep. We were going to call a cab but Yvette reminded me that we were being adventurous. She snatched the keys to the Blazer and we slipped out in the morning. We slapped each other a high five as we drove back to the club to get our car. Once there, we left the keys on the front seat and I wrote "Thanks for the fuck!" in red lipstick on the front windshield.

15

olive

"Listen up, sorors. I know we had decided to keep the D.C. chapter enrollment of APF to a minimum, but I'd like to make a nomination." We'd just gathered at a secret location for our monthly freak night. We were waiting for the cum daddies to arrive. That's my personal nickname for them and now it seems to be becoming popular among the sorors.

"Nomination?" Soror Yolanda asked, obviously disturbed by the mere thought.

"She better be the mofo bomb diggity because I like things just the way they are," Soror Keisha interjected.

"You all just hear Olive out!" Patricia started yelling at the group. She has this thing about people getting sassy with me since I brought her into the group. "She's our elected leader so give her some respect."

Keisha smacked her lips and threw daggers at me with her eyes. "We're listening, but this better be good."

"You've all met her before," I continued. "At our investment club meeting a couple of months ago."

"You have got to be shittin' me!" Yvette exclaimed. "You're not talking about that countrified chick from school, are you?" She frowned at Patricia. "The one that was in the dining hall with you that day?"

Patricia quickly responded. "Yes, we are, and she has a name."

"Her name's Mary Ann Ferguson," I announced. "She's originally from South Dakota, she's a straight-A student, and she's definitely APF material."

Soror Melanie was the next one to voice an objection. "We agreed that our membership was closed unless someone truly exceptional happened to come along."

"I believe that Mary Ann is truly exceptional," I stated vehemently. "So does Patricia. Right, soror?"

"Absolutely." Patricia got up and stood beside me in unity. "I stand behind Mary Ann's nomination one hundred percent."

"My nomination stands." I took a quick survey of the faces in the room. Melanie, Lisa, and most of the others would go along with me. I wasn't too sure about Yvette or Keisha. As for Yolanda, she knew better not to even try me. If it wasn't for me, her ass wouldn't be there either. It was getting dangerously close to the time for the cum daddies to arrive and we needed to get into fuck mode. "Shall we take a vote before the men get here?"

16

mary ann

I really had mixed feelings about spending Thanksgiving with Trevor. We were back on speaking terms but that was about it. He swore up and down that I was the only one for him. Every time that crap came out of his mouth, I made it a point to remind him of the night FeFe was over there waxing his dick.

Trevor promised that if I spent Thanksgiving with him, it would be a night I would never forget. I had to admit that it sounded intriguing. After the experiences I'd had with Drayton, I couldn't imagine something being more unforgettable. Especially in light of the fact that Trevor had never actually blown my mind in bed.

Besides, I couldn't afford to go home. Daddy had promised me that he would send me a plane ticket to come home for Christmas and I could hardly wait. I had never flown before and half of me was terrified. The other half was excited. All my life I had watched movies with people flying the friendly skies and it looked like a lot of fun. Then again, the thought of plummeting twenty thousand feet to earth if something went wrong wasn't appealing at all.

Trevor didn't want to go home for some reason. I got the impression that he wasn't very close to his parents. From what I could see, he rarely called them. Only once did he say he had to go home because of an emergency. Otherwise he never mentioned going home for a visit. Trevor came from money and was the typical spoiled little rich boy. He was used to getting whatever he wanted and that probably explained his tendency to run through women right and left. I was now determined that he would never make a fool out of me again. If anything, I would be the one to make a fool out of him.

Dinner was romantic and nice, but I wouldn't call it unforgettable. Trevor picked me up from my dorm, which was practically abandoned, and drove me out to Alexandria, Virginia, to an upscale rooftop restaurant on top of a resort hotel. The view of the city from there was gorgeous. The restaurant was packed, it was a good thing he made reservations. I thought everybody ate Thanksgiving dinner at home, like they did back home. Apparently, that was not the case in the D.C. area.

"What's on your mind, Mary Ann?" Trevor asked once the waitress had taken our drink order.

I grinned at him. "What makes you think there's anything on my mind?"

"Because you're so quiet."

"I really don't have much to talk about."

"You were silent in the car on the way over here too."

I shrugged. "Sorry if I'm bad company."

Trevor reached across the white linen tablecloth and took my hand. "Look, I have apologized over and over again about what happened."

I rolled my eyes and yanked my hand away.

"I made a mistake and I admit it. It will never happen again."

"Maybe it's just your nature."

He sighed. "I'll admit that there was a time, in my youth, when I thought it was my duty to satisfy more than one woman at once."

I had to grab the cloth napkin and cough into it to prevent myself from laughing. Satisfy women, my ass! Trevor was not working with half the amount of sexual skills that he assumed he was.

"When I first got to law school, women were throwing themselves at me right and left. I wasn't in love or attached or anything like that, so I did what every red-blooded American man would do. I made the most of the situation."

I felt myself getting angry. "Did you ever consider the feelings of the women you were *satisfying?*"

"Yes, of course. I know you find that hard to believe, but I always considered their feelings."

"And what about my feelings when you hooked back up with FeFe?"

The waitress returned with Trevor's screwdriver and my strawberry daiquiri. I could tell from the expression on his face that Trevor was relieved to get a few seconds to come up with a response.

"Are you ready to order?" she asked.

"Can you give us a few more minutes?" I responded. "I haven't had a chance to read the entire menu."

"Sure. Just so you know, our special tonight is roasted turkey breast with apple-walnut dressing, gravy, sweet potatoes, and collard greens."

"Wow, sounds like back home."

Trevor chuckled. "Not bad for a ritzy place, huh?"

I laughed in return. "No, it's a good thing. I thought we would have to end up eating duckling or something."

The waitress was about to leave but we stopped her and ordered two specials. There was no need to peruse the menu when the special was on point.

I decided to let Trevor off the hook and not bring up FeFe again. I refused to let thoughts of her nasty behind ruin my Thanksgiving dinner. By sitting there discussing her, I was letting her win and get the results she had hoped for. That was not going to happen.

Trevor actually made me laugh throughout dinner and that was refreshing because I had been wound up pretty tight lately. School was going well, although I could have done without the company and attitude of a couple of my professors. I couldn't wait until the spring term so I could get them out of my life. The study load was outrageous but I knew that it would be before I came. It was all part of the challenge, a challenge I craved.

After dinner, Trevor excused himself from the table. I thought he was going to the men's room, but after he was gone more than ten minutes, I grew concerned. All sorts of silly thoughts started running through my mind like whether he had crept off to call another woman to make plans for the rest of the night, or to cancel them.

He came back to the table full of apologies.

"Sorry it took me so long."

"Is your stomach all right?" I asked.

"Yes, my stomach is fine. I just went down to the lobby to take care of something."

"What's down in the lobby?"

"The registration desk." He chugged down the last of his third screwdriver. "It may have been presumptuous of me but I decided to see if they had an available room for tonight."

Hmph, he thought he was going to get some booty. Not!

"Well, I hope you didn't get a room because I was definitely planning on going back to my dorm tonight."

"Aw, damn! The only room they had left was a deluxe suite and I already charged it. It was quite pricey too."

"Then you can drop me off at the dorm and come back here and spend the night."

The look on Trevor's face was priceless. "Mary Ann, you're really not playing fair."

"I didn't realize we were playing a game, Trevor."

"You know what I mean. I realize you're probably not ready to be intimate with me again but that doesn't mean we can't cuddle."

I snickered. "Cuddle? I didn't realize men use that word."

"You get my drift."

We sat there arguing over the matter until Trevor wore me down and everyone that had ordered around the same time as us was long gone. I agreed to go to the suite with him so he would shut the hell up.

The suite was incredible. I had never seen anything like it. The bed was big enough for five or six people and the dark cherry furniture reeked of money. The bathroom was huge, the size of regular hotel rooms, and had a marble Jacuzzi. Trevor insisted on running me a bath. A bath was exactly what I needed but I made it clear that I would only be bathing. Trevor didn't try to impose and that was a smart move on his part. He caught something on cable while I enjoyed the jets spraying warm water all over my body. I had never had that experience before and now I knew why so many people made a fuss over Jacuzzis.

In fact, the water hitting up against my breasts and pussy made me horny. The lights in the bathroom were dimmed and I wished that Drayton, or someone as well endowed as he, was in there with me. I closed my eyes and conjured him up. Then I fingered myself until I had a toe-curling orgasm.

Too bad for Trevor. If he was hoping to bust a nut that night, he was on his own because I had already gotten mine.

patricia

Thanksgiving is a special time of the year for most people. Thanksgiving for me was a rebirth every year. I lost my virginity on Thanksgiving Day. I was seventeen years old and it was in the back seat of Zander Turner's Trans Am. There was barely enough room to lift my legs but we somehow managed and that night changed my life.

Zander got married to Gina, a girl he had been dealing with most of his life, right after high school. Damn shame because he and I belonged together. His marriage was practically arranged. Zander's mother and Gina's mother had been best friends for close to thirty years, so they forced the kids together while they were still in diapers. Gina might have been a decent woman and she was the mother of Zander's three children but that still didn't stop his one addiction: me.

For a while after the marriage, I played the serious mistress role. We fucked every chance we got, including the day before his wedding and the day he returned from his honeymoon. He almost didn't make it to the wedding rehearsal because he didn't want to pull himself away from my pussy. I never felt like it was a dirty thing. Zander and I were a natural. A spontaneous combustion whenever we were in the same room. I find it hard to believe that Gina never figured it out. Where the hell did she think he was late at night?

I grew tired of it, owning the dick but not owning the man. I knew breaking it off was the right thing to do but the thought of never fucking him again was too much. Thus, we came to an agreement. Every Thanksgiving we fuck the taste out of each other's mouths.

I go home to New York to eat Thanksgiving dinner with my parents and afterward, Zander and I meet at the Marriott Marquis in Times Square to get our freak on. Where he tells Gina he's going every year, I have no idea. My parents have never been the type to question me, but they are not stupid either.

Zander looked especially fine that Thanksgiving when he knocked on the door of Room 1320. He was wearing a pair of black slacks and a form-fitting ivory sweater. He looked like he'd just stepped off the pages of a men's fashion magazine. Zander is tall, dark, and always clean-shaven. His black, silky hair always felt great rubbing against my inner thighs.

"Hey, baby," I cooed as I opened the door so he could come in. I was slightly hidden because I didn't want to chance someone walking down the hallway seeing me in all my naked glory.

Zander's eyes widened when he realized I was already nude. "Glad to see I don't have to waste any time undressing you."

We both laughed as I jumped into his arms and straddled my legs around his waist. I slipped my tongue in his mouth. "Umm, you taste sweet."

"No, that's all you, Patricia. My sweet, sweet thing."

I decided to tease him. "You're not going to feel guilty this year, are you?"

He tossed me on the bed and started undressing with a quickness. "Do I look like I feel guilty?"

When he dropped his pants, his dick was at full attention.

"No, you look like you could split bricks with that thing."

He spread my legs and climbed on top of me. "I'd rather split you wide open with it."

"Do the damn thing, then."

And do the damn thing, he did.

17

mary ann

After my freaky experiences with Drayton, you would think I would have been prepared for anything. Well, that's what I thought—until Olive showed up at my door one night in a long trench coat with a hat concealing her face. I jokingly asked her if she was on an undercover mission.

"Something like that," she said.

She demanded that I put on some dark clothing and a base-ball cap and meet her down in the car. Strange, I thought. I reluctantly agreed and within minutes we were on our way somewhere in downtown D.C. near the waterfront. She was driving a rental car, instead of her Jaguar. Things were getting straight up spooky.

I thought it was strange that Olive would come get me in the first place. It isn't like we were friends. We sexually had a man in common. But as far as I knew, she didn't even know about my second rendezvous with Drayton. Something inside of me was curious enough to follow Olive's lead. I was hoping great sex would be somewhere in the picture.

I asked Olive over and over where we were going, especially when we passed a group of winos sharing a bottle. They stood around a trash barrel with a blazing fire—as if the liquor wouldn't keep them warm enough. Olive's response to my queries was to ignore me and crank up the volume of the music playing in the car. It was reggae so I just gyrated my hips to the music and relaxed. I felt a sharp pain shoot up my spine, though, when she parked in front of what appeared to be an abandoned warehouse.

"Um Olive, are you sure this is safe?" I asked. I was scared to get out of the car.

"It's cool. Just trust me," she replied, cutting the engine and hopping out of the car.

We walked up to a door, which had a huge metal knocker on it. Olive lifted it and dropped it against the door three times.

She got an instant response. "Who's there?" a husky male voice demanded to know from the other side of the door.

"The Dick Lover!" she shouted back at him.

"What's the password?"

"Anal-retentive!"

I fell out laughing. "You've got to be kidding!"

A small peephole in the door opened briefly and I didn't see anything but an eyeball. Next thing you know, the door swung open.

"Come on in, ladies," a tall, handsome brotha said, extending an invitation.

It was extremely dark in the place and I grabbed onto Olive's elbow so I wouldn't tumble down the flight of stairs directly inside the door.

"What the hell is this place, Olive?"

She looked at me, grinned and said, "Heaven!"

When we reached the bottom of the stairs, I had to repeat, "What the hell is this place?"

Olive grabbed my hand and pulled me farther into the room. "I already told you. It's heaven!" It was a huge room filled with naked people. Men and women were fucking each other right and left, and some were engaged with multiple partners. I had heard of orgies but it was nothing like seeing one.

One man brushed past me and grabbed my ass. I practically jumped out of my boots. "Olive, I don't think I feel comfortable here. Can we go?"

She chuckled. "We just got here." She moved away from me and started dancing to the house music that was blaring from the speakers built into the walls. "Relax. No one is going to make you do anything you don't want to do. You can just watch if you want. I know how much you like that. Remember how much seeing Drayton and me fucking turned you on?"

I nodded. "Yes, I remember."

She swung around in a circle with her arms extended. "Well, then you really should be in heaven here because you can watch all these people fuck for as long as you want to."

I pointed behind me. "But that man just grabbed my ass."

"Did you think he was cute?"

I shrugged. "Maybe."

Olive came closer to me and brushed my hair behind my ears with her fingers. "Mary Ann, we only live once and we have to make that one time count. Life is so stressful. Everyone deserves a way to relax. These are all good people here. No one wants to harm you or make you feel ashamed. There is no shame in this room. Only pleasure."

"But what about diseases?" I asked in a panic.

"Condoms exist for a reason," Olive replied, pulling a handful of them out of her coat pocket. "And I came prepared."

I glanced around the room and zeroed in on a sister in the far corner that was sucking one man's dick and being fucked from behind by another one. The look on her face was pure ecstasy and it turned me on big time. I still couldn't help but ask, "Why did you bring me here?"

Olive smiled and started unbuttoning her coat. "Honestly?"

"Yes."

She let her coat fall from her shoulders and she was buck naked underneath. I couldn't help but envy her body. She held one of the condoms in her hand. "I brought you here as a test."

"A test?"

"Yes, I believe in tests. Drayton was also a test."

"I'm confused."

A tall man walked up behind Olive and started palming her breasts. She moaned and started swaying her hips in unison with him. "Is the man behind me fine?"

I looked at the man, not believing that she would let some-one feel her up that she had never even seen. He had sexy eyes and a wickedly handsome smile. "Yes, he is," I replied.

Olive giggled. "Good. I think I'll fuck him then." She slightly turned her head toward him and closed her eyes, hand-ing him the condom. "One rule. I don't want to see your face. That would take all the fun out of it."

He laughed and started kissing her shoulders, lowering himself onto his knees and biting on her ass cheeks.

Olive looked at me. "Mary Ann, one day soon I am going to come to you and make you a proposition."

"What type of proposition?"

"One you hopefully can't refuse."

"And if I do refuse?"

Olive walked over to a nearby table and bent over it. The man followed, slapped on the condom, and quickly entered her from behind.

"Mary Ann, if you refuse, then everything is still everything. No hard feelings."

I was still totally confused, but decided that whatever she was talking about would become clear in time. Besides, watch-ing the man fuck her only made me more aroused than I already was.

She pointed behind me. "Your friend is back and, I must say; he's holding."

I turned around and took him in with my eyes. He was in-deed one of the finest men I had ever laid eyes on. He had this exotic look going on.

He whispered in my ear, "Tell me your fantasy."

"Well," I heard Olive call from behind me. "What do you plan to do?"

I felt the guy up and my right hand landed on his dick. He was fully erect and something told me, merely by the way he eyed me, that he could satisfy the cravings inside of me.

I picked up Olive's coat. "Let me borrow one of these condoms."

olive

"So what the hell happened?"

I had barely had time to sit down on my sofa before Patricia started grilling me.

"Come on, spill the beans!" she insisted. I rolled my eyes.

"Could you calm down, please?"

Patricia rolled her eyes back. "I just want to know what happened. You were the one that insisted I shouldn't go."

"That's because I was convinced Mary Ann wouldn't open up around you. At least, not yet. She seems to have some high level of regard for you; as if you aren't a big ass freak like the rest of us. If she only knew the real deal."

Patricia grimaced. "Cute, real cute."

"Seriously. It's like she's afraid of you judging her or something."

"Well, she's just going to have to get over that."

"I think she will. All in good time." I took a sip of my piña colada and held the glass toward Patricia. "Want one? I just blended them."

"No, thank you. What I want is some information and I'd like it sometime today."

"There's no reason to be brutal." I sat there twirling my straw for a minute, more to irritate Patricia than to mix my drink. I finally decided to put her out of her misery. "I took her to Heaven, just like I'd planned."

"And? Did she freak out?"

"Not in the way you use the term. She did some serious fucking though."

"You're kidding."

"I never kid about such things."

"I'm just shocked."

"Why would you be shocked? You were the one that first came to me and said she fit the APF profile. Now that we know it for sure, you're suprised?"

Patricia got up and paced the floor. "So, how many men did she fuck?"

"I lost count."

"Get the fuck out of here!"

"Okay, it wasn't that deep but I know she did at least two. One in the main room and one in the hot tub."

"Any women?"

"No, I don't think Mary Ann gets down like that."

Patricia disappeared into the kitchen for a couple of minutes and came back with a piña colada. I knew she would go for one because I'd never seen her turn down a drink.

After sitting beside me on the sofa, she asked, "So it's time then?"

I sighed. "The timing will never get any better than this."

18

patricia

"Mary Ann. Patricia. Come right on in." Olive beamed at us, moving out of the way so we could cross her threshold. "I've prepared some jambalaya and made some frozen piña coladas."

"Sounds good," I said, rubbing my belly. I hadn't had a thing to eat all day and I was a huge fan of Olive's piña coladas. Never turned them down.

"Yes, it does sound nice." Mary Ann followed us into the living room. "Thanks for inviting me."

"You're always welcome in my home, Mary Ann."

Olive and Mary Ann stared each other down for a few seconds. "Thank you."

"All of these thank-yous are really not necessary," Olive said, heading into the kitchen to get us some drinks.

Mary Ann and I sat down on the sofa. She leaned into me and whispered, "I'm just trying to be polite."

We stuffed our bellies full of delicious jambalaya. I got a bit tipsy off the piña coladas and spent the majority of the evening trying to think of the correct approach to the matter at hand.

"Mary Ann, there's something important Olive and I need to discuss with you," I blurted out, interrupting a hand of trump between the two of them.

She gave me the most incredulous look before responding. "Is this about what happened between Drayton and me? I only went back to his place that one time."

"Say what? When did you go back over there?" Olive demanded to know. From the frying pan into the fire, I thought.

"I'm sorry. I just assumed he told you," Mary Ann whispered apologetically. She pleaded for Olive's forgiveness with her eyes. When she didn't get a positive response, she glared back at me. "Anyway, I take it you know what happened, Patricia? About what happened in the alley that day and the next night? I can tell by the way you've been acting toward me."

I was cold busted and I knew it. "Olive did mention it."

"I bet," Mary Ann hissed. "Did she tell you about the club also?"

I shrugged, ignoring the question. "That's not what we brought you here to discuss." I braced myself for the next statement. I had no idea what Mary Ann's reaction would be. "It's about our investment club."

"Oh, is that all?" she snidely remarked, appearing slightly relieved. "I've been thinking quite a bit about that and if it's okay I'd like to invest a few dollars every month."

I glanced over at Olive, making sure she'd take up the slack for me if things turned ugly. She had this special way of explaining things that none of the rest of us were blessed with. She nodded, urging me to continue. "That's cool, but there's a little more to the club than that."

"Like?"

"You remember Yvette?" I asked, knowing good and damn well she did. "The sistah that called me soror in the dining hall that day?"

"Yes, she's a friend of yours from high school." Mary Ann took another sip of her piña colada. "She was also here at the meeting that day, right?"

"Yes, but she's not a friend from high school. She's not even from New York. I lied." A quizzical look overtook Mary Ann's face. "I met Yvette through Olive."

Mary Ann darted her eyes over at Olive and then back at me. "I don't understand what you're trying to tell me."

"You see, Yvette and I are sorors, but not because of some girls' club in high school. We belong to . . . I mean, we're both a part of . . ." I started searching for words that wouldn't come. That's when Olive took over.

"Let me handle this, sissypoo." Olive got up off the floor, walked around the coffee table, and sat down next to Mary Ann on the sofa. "Mary Ann, I believe in calling a spade a spade, a dick a dick, and a pussy a pussy."

Mary Ann cackled and so did I. Olive sure did have a way with words. "Your point being?"

"Patricia, Yvette, and all the other women that were here in my place that first day belong to the D.C. chapter of a nation-wide secret sorority."

"What's a secret sorority?" Mary Ann asked.

"One that only the members know about," she replied. "Ac-tually, there are nonmembers who know. The men we invite to freak nights."

Mary Ann chuckled. Some of her drink trickled out the sides of her mouth. "Did you just say freak nights?"

"The way it basically works is that two sorors are selected each month at our investment club meeting to organize freak night for that month, which generally occurs the last Saturday of every month. We meet in a secret location, not at any of our actual homes, and then do a bunch of freaky-deaky shit."

"And they find the men?"

"Yes, whoever is in charge of freak night picks the men."

"What if you're not attracted to the men?" Mary Ann chided.

"They're all very attractive," Olive interjected. "We're ex-tremely picky and I've never been disappointed with the dick selections."

"Let me get this straight," she blurted out at one point. "You guys meet up with strange men one day out of every month and have sex with them?"

"Hellz yeah!" Olive shouted, her ghettoized twin appearing. "We fuck them and it's all good too!"

"And you never see these men again?"

"We never see them again," I replied. "They never know our real names or what any of us do for a living or anything like that. We just use them for sex and then send them on their way. Similar to what we did at the club but APF is on a whole other level."

"But, but, but how do you find thcm?"

"We find our cum daddies everywhere," Olive answered.

Mary Ann fell out laughing. "Cum daddies? This is getting wilder by the second."

We spent the next three hours telling Mary Ann all about Alpha Phi Fuckem Sorority, Inc.

We told her how the founding members started it in the late seventies right in D.C. and how we'd spread out into seven different chapters: D.C., New York City, Chicago, Los Angeles, Detroit, Atlanta, and Miami.

We described our philosophy, our goals, our mission statement.

"Olive, what about you and Drayton?"

Olive guffawed. "Drayton doesn't even know my real name. Neither do you for that matter." She reached out her hand to shake Mary Ann's. "My real name is Olive Cooper."

"I knew Cox sounded kinda bogus." Mary Ann giggled. "I find it hard to believe all of this. This is just too incredible."

"It's incredibly fun," I teased. "Alpha Phi Fuckem has changed my life."

"I can't do this. I'm with Trevor."

"You didn't seem too hung up on Trevor the other night when you were getting busy with manwhore number one and manwhore number two. Besides, I have a boyfriend too."

"You mean, other than Drayton?"

"Yes, his name is Hakim. He travels quite a bit on business but you'll meet him eventually. Now that you know my real name and all."

We all shared a laugh.

"Will you tell me what you do for a living now?" Mary Ann asked.

"I'm a plastic surgeon."

"Really?" Mary Ann squealed.

"Yes, I've made a shitload of money off people wanting to look better."

"I could tell you were smart."

"We're all smart. All of the sorors are either highly regarded professionals or well on their way like Patricia, Yvette, and yourself."

"That's why keeping our identities sacred is so important," I added. "Most of the sorors have significant others and a few are even married."

"Married?" Mary Ann fidgeted on the sofa. "And their husbands don't suspect something foul is going on?"

"Nope." I joined them on the sofa, sitting on the opposite side of Mary Ann from Olive. "Listen, Mary Ann, we're not trying to pressure you into making a rash decision tonight or anything, but it's quite obvious Trevor isn't knocking the bottom out of that pussy." She glared at me with disdain. "Then again, I knew that already. I tried to warn you."

"Let's not discuss my sex life with Trevor," Mary Ann snarled. "That's personal between the two of us."

Olive played referee. "Enough about some damn Trevor. Let's talk about Alpha Phi Fuckem." Mary Ann and I both fell silent. "Mary Ann, if you're down with this, all you have to do is let us know. There's no shame in our game. We are what we are. Sexually uninhibited women that like to get fucked right once a month. Hakim's my heart and soul but he doesn't fulfill all of my physical needs so I get my jollies off elsewhere."

"Can I just have some time to think about this?" Mary Ann asked, gulping down her sixth or seventh piña colada. "This is a lot to ingest in one night."

"Take as long as you want," I responded, placing my hand on her knee for reassurance.

"I tell you what, Mary Ann," Olive said. "The next freak night is in two weeks. Give it some thought and let us know what you decide."

"Okay," Mary Ann whispered. "I'll do that."

19

mary ann

What a day! Patricia and Olive had really thrown me into a tailspin by inviting me to join Alpha Phi Fuckem. I had never heard of such a thing but I guess that was the point. They were unique and I had to admit that I was flattered they would even consider me APF material. After all, a sexpot I was not. I had just done a few wild things with Olive but nothing of the nature they were describing.

I had just entered the dorm when I heard someone yelling my name.

"Mary Ann! Mary Ann! Over here!"

I couldn't believe my eyes when I spotted Clarence standing in the middle of the lobby waving. "Oh, my God!" I exclaimed. It was like seeing a ghost.

"Mary Ann, I almost didn't recognize you," Clarence said, rushing toward me. "What's with the new clothes?"

I had on a white blouse, red sweater, and black tweed skirt. There was nothing spectacular about what I had on but it was a lot different from the way he was used to seeing me.

"Um, Clarence, what are you doing here?"

"I came to see you." He reached me and flung his arms around me, almost taking the wind out of me. "What do you think I'm doing here?"

"But, but why?" I asked, pushing him away from me. "We haven't even talked lately."

"I know and I felt really bad about that." Clarence put his hands in his overall pockets and eyed the floor. "I decided to hop in my truck and come see you."

"You drove all the way here?"

"Yeah, I was scared shitless though. You know my truck isn't in the best shape but I just had to see you."

I laughed. His truck was on its last legs. I was shocked it even made it out of the state.

I eyed him up and down. Clarence did still look good, or maybe I was just so used to the way he looked. Some of the feelings for him came flooding back but I had not forgotten the day I called and Jessica answered, throwing the fact that she was sleeping with him up in my face.

"What about Jessica?" I asked angrily.

He shrugged but kept his eyes on the floor. "What about her?"

"Oh, so now you're going to play dumb? You know exactly what I'm talking about."

"Jessica was just something that happened. I was kind of bitter when you picked law school over me."

I shook my head in disgust. "It wasn't even like that."

"Well, whatever it was like, it wasn't fair."

"Clarence, that's selfish. I made a choice to pursue a dream and it had absolutely nothing to do with choosing one thing over the other."

"If you say so."

"Anyway, that's all a moot point now because we're history."

"Mary Ann, I came all the way here. Can we at least sit down somewhere and have a heart-to-heart talk?"

I pointed to a nearby sofa in the lobby sitting area. "We can sit right here."

"What about someplace more private?" He looked around. It was rather crowded. A lot of people were heading out for a Friday night on the town. "Why don't we grab a bite to eat? Wherever you want. My treat."

I really didn't want to go anywhere with Clarence but taking him up to my room wasn't an option. On second thought, sitting in the lobby wasn't such a good idea either. All I needed was for Trevor to show up to make the drama in my day even thicker.

"Okay. We can go someplace to eat." I started walking toward the front entrance. "You still like ribs?"

"Yeah, I love ribs. You know that."

"I thought I knew everything about you, Clarence. Apparently, a lot of things changed the moment I left town."

He put his arm around my waist and kissed me on the cheek. "Some things never change, Mary Ann. Even if we want them to."

"Hmph!" I pulled away from him and pushed the door open. "Please refrain from touching me," I said nastily.

Clarence shook his head. "Oh, so it's like that?"

"Absolutely."

About thirty minutes later, we arrived at the Capital City Brewing Company. I had been there one other time with Trevor and I knew the ribs were slamming. They slow-roasted ribs over an open flame for hours, they didn't come any tenderer. I also knew that Clarence liked to down beers and they had a special selection on tap. I really don't know why I was even trying to accommodate his likes; catering to people was a habit and I needed to stop.

Five minutes later we had a table. We ordered and our food came quickly.

"Umph, umph, umph!" Clarence said, washing down a mouthful of ribs with a German beer. "You weren't lying when you said the ribs were delicious here."

"I'm glad you like them. But, we really need to talk. After all, that was our main purpose in coming. Right?" I said.

"Yeah." Clarence belched, and didn't even bother to say "excuse me." Disgusting. I guess once men feel comfortable around a woman, belching, farting, and other bodily noises don't even warrant an "excuse me."

"So what exactly did you want to talk about, Clarence?" I asked, trying to get the evening over as soon as possible.

He flashed the grin that used to make me melt. "Us, of course."

"There is no us. Like I said back at my dorm, we're history."

"We're not history. We have a lot of history behind us and that's why we can't just let it go."

"Is that what you were thinking when you were fucking Jessica?"

Clarence almost choked on a rib. "I've never heard you talk like that before. City life must be dirtying up your mouth."

I felt myself getting angrier. "Clarence, I'm grown and I have been for a long time. If I want to use the word *fuck* and any other curse word, that's my damn business."

Clarence threw his hands up in the air and pushed his palms toward me. "Whoa, no need to get nasty. I just meant that I've never heard you curse before."

"Well, now you have. Mark the date down in your calendar." Clarence sighed and took another sip of his beer. He must have realized that talking to me wasn't going to be as easy as he thought. "I drove all this way to see you because I want to set things straight. It took me what seemed like an eternity and three tanks of gas to get here. Can we at least be civil?"

I rolled my eyes. Maybe he had a point. I should at least hear him out, even though I knew there wasn't a snowball's chance in hell that he would make me view him any differently.

"Clarence, I apologize for being *nasty*. I just wasn't expecting to see you today. This came out of the clear blue. You sent my stuff back to me, what little there was of it, and made it obvious that you were the one done with me."

"What if I'm not done?" he asked. "What if I'm still madly in love with you?"

"That would be unfortunate." I took a deep breath and decided to come clean. "I've moved on. I have someone new in my life."

The expression on Clarence's face was indescribable. You would have thought someone slapped him. "What do you mean, you have someone new in your life?"

"His name's Trevor. Trevor Ames. I'm planning on moving in with him next semester."

"Moving in with him?" Clarence slammed his fist down on the table, causing our plates to jump a little. "I asked you to move in with me at least fifty times and you said it would be inappropriate. Now you've been here less than six months and you're about to shack up with a fool you barely know."

"First off, Trevor is not a fool. He's in his third year of law school and he's one of the smartest students in the entire school. Secondly, it would have been inappropriate for me to move in with you when my parents were so close by and needed my help with the kids."

"Oh please, that's just a bunch of baloney. Why are you doing this, Mary Ann?"

I couldn't help but laugh. "Clarence, you're acting like some innocent victim. I wasn't even planning on seriously dating Trevor until I called you that day and Jessica was playing house with you."

"I already explained that Jessica was a mistake. I was upset."

"Poor baby, but that's not an excuse."

Suddenly, I wanted Clarence to feel pain. Maybe pain he didn't deserve, considering my sexual escapades of late, but I wanted him to feel it just the same.

"Clarence, Trevor has made me realize just what I was missing sexually," I lied. "He has taken me to heights I never knew existed and I feel like a new woman."

Clarence looked like he was on the brink of tears. "Are you saying that I'm a lousy lay?"

"I'm saying that until recently, you were my *only* lay and now I realize what else is out there. I've gone through a sexual transformation, so to speak."

"And this Trevor fool is responsible for it?"

"In some ways, yes. In many ways, no."

"You're not making any sense."

"How is everything?" our waitress asked, appearing out of nowhere. "Can I get you another beer?" she asked Clarence.

He was too shocked to respond so I said, "Everything's fine. Thank you."

"Just answer me one thing," Clarence said after the waitress had walked away. "How long did it take you to give it up to him?"

"Why does that matter?"

"It just does."

"Quite honestly, I didn't sleep with Trevor right away. I wasn't even sure I liked him. But he grew on me."

"He grew on you?"

"Yes." I cleared my throat. "And then there were the others. Now them I did give it up to quickly. Basically on sight."

"What the fuck are you talking about?" Clarence yelled at me.

People started looking in our direction and I just grinned toward the bar and winked at one man sitting there alone. He turned his head, not knowing how to react.

"Mary Ann, answer me, dammit!"

"Now look who's cursing like a sailor," I said jokingly. "What do you think I'm talking about? Trevor is not the only man I've been with since I moved to D.C."

"How many of them have there been?"

"I don't remember." That was partially true because I wasn't sure how many men I'd allowed to penetrate me at Heaven. "But all of them have taught me something."

"Mary Ann, you disgust me. Do your parents know you moved here to become a common whore?"

"I'm not a whore. I'm sexually liberated and it's about time too."

"You are a whore and if your parents don't know it, then someone should tell them. Maybe it'll be me."

"And maybe you'll end up with my foot up your ass," I said with disdain. "You are not my overseer and I don't owe you a damn thing. Not another chance, not an explanation, nothing. I didn't ask you to come see me. In fact, you make me sick and I don't even want you here."

Clarence stood up and looked down at me. "I'll tell you what. No one needs your ass anyway. I'm in D.C. and I didn't come all this way to hear this bullshit. I'm going to find me a booty club, I know they have a ton of them here, and find me a freak to get with tonight. I'm going to get laid, even if I have to pay for it."

I chuckled. "As sorry as you are in bed, you're going to have to pay for it."

"Bitch, pay for your own dinner!"

Clarence stormed out the door without even looking back in my direction. I waved the waitress over to get the check and she was visibly nervous. After paying her, I got up to leave and was halfway out the door when something came over me.

I glanced at the bar and the same man I'd winked at earlier was still sitting there. I had barely noticed it before but he was strikingly handsome. He was much older than me, probably in his late forties, but time had obviously been kind to him. He was a deep chocolate with dark bedroom eyes and a bald head.

There was a vacant stool beside him at the bar so I snatched it up. "Excuse me, but can I ask you a question?"

He looked me up and down before replying, "Sure, shoot."

"Did you witness that little episode that just took place over there?"

He chortled. "It would have been kind of hard not to notice it. The two of you were rather loud."

"Did you hear what he called me?"

"I heard him call you a bitch before he ran out of here."

"Hmm, what about the other thing he called me?"

He looked down at his beer. "Can I buy you a drink?"

"Sure, as soon as you give me an honest answer."

"I heard the word *whore* being thrown around once or twice."

"Do I look like a whore to you?"

He laughed. "I've been around the block a time or two and I couldn't tell you what a whore looks like. Some women are perceived as whores that aren't and others that look like pure innocence are banging everybody."

I gently caressed his arm. "You're a wise man."

"I don't know about wisdom. It's more like experience. I was once married to a woman that played that innocent role."

"But she wasn't innocent?"

"Ha, that's the understatement of the century. She was pretending to go out every night to work as a home aide and she was really strolling street corners."

I was stunned. "You mean she was a hooker?"

"The hooker of all hookers."

"That's amazing."

He stared at me strangely. "You almost say that like you admire it."

"No, not at all. I don't think exchanging money for sex is a good thing. Although there is something to be said for sex with strangers. But only if the chemistry is mutual."

"You're a tough one to figure out."

"Why do you say that?"

"You walk in here with someone who looks like he just got off a tractor, yet you seem sophisticated and intelligent. He lays you out, walks out on you, and now you're sitting here doing something that seems like flirting with me."

He was right about one thing. I could barely figure out what was going through my head myself. The earlier lengthy conversation with Patricia and Olive about APF was still messing with me, and then there was Clarence's appearance. I should have gotten up and taken my behind back to school to study or, better yet, called Trevor to come get me so he and I could try to sort out some things. Instead, I was sitting there contemplating fucking the shit out of an older stranger who was probably just trying to enjoy a few beers and go home.

"Is that offer for a drink still on the table?" I asked.

He grinned and looked quite sexy while doing it. "Sure. What will it be?"

I leaned over and whispered in his ear. "How about an orgasm?"

He waved the bartender over and that began a two-hour flirt session.

20

olive

Patricia left shortly after Mary Ann, claiming she had to go study. On a Friday night? I knew her ass better than that but it was cool. Hakim's plane had just landed from Hong Kong and I was anxious to see him. So much so that I called him on his cell phone and told him to wait for me at National Airport.

After I met him at baggage claim, we snuck into a stall of one of the restrooms with a Closed for Cleaning sign out front and did each other in one of the stalls. Certain people have one thing that turns them on more than anything else. Having sex in public places had always been mine. I guess that's why they called me Soror Unrestricted. Patricia's thing was threesomes, foursomes, or the more the merrier. That's why we called her

Soror Ménage à Trois. Then there was Soror Cum Hard who had more orgasms than seemed humanly possible, Soror Cheeks who loved to go down on men, and Soror Three Input who loved the hell out of anal sex. We were quite the eclectic mix.

Hakim and I ended up having dinner at a cozy spot in Georgetown. It was well-known around the area for its crab cakes. I enjoyed the atmosphere just as much as the food.

"So Olive, were you a good girl while I was gone?" Hakim asked me over dessert.

I batted my eyelashes and smiled at him. "I'm always a good girl when you're gone. What would make you think otherwise?"

He waved his finger at me. "Uh-huh, I know you. I love you. I worship the ground you walk on. I also know that you're an undercover freak."

I laughed. "An undercover freak?"

"Yes, you have a sex appetite out of this world. Sometimes I wonder how you go so long without sex while I'm away."

Hakim was looking especially fine that night. He was wearing a tailored black designer suit with a cream shirt and paisley tie.

I took his hand. "Baby, when you're away, I simply satisfy myself. You know I masturbate all the time."

He grinned at me. "Boy, don't I know it. I love it when you do it in front of me. Often, I feel like you love your toys more than me."

"No, that'll never happen. Not in a million years."

He lifted my hand to his mouth and kissed my fingers. "If you say so."

The white linen tablecloth reached down to the floor so I slipped off my shoe, found his dick, and started giving him a foot job. No sooner had he started moaning than I spotted Drayton walking in the door with two other men.

"Oh shit," I whispered.

"What's wrong?" Hakim asked.

"Um, nothing." I took my foot down and put it back in my shoe.

"Why'd you stop? I was getting off on that."

"I know but I just had this sudden pain in my stomach. I hope I'm not getting ulcers."

"Damn, baby, I hope not either," Hakim said in a panic. "Has work been stressing you out lately?"

"No, not really." I kept my eye on Drayton and his party. Luckily, all the tables were taken and they were ushered to the bar to wait for one. "I've had a little trouble sleeping though. My parents are going at it again and Mom is always calling me to tell her side of the story."

"You want to catch a flight to San Francisco to check on her? I'll go with you."

"I can't. My schedule is too tight right now. Christmas is coming up and everyone wants to look their best for the holidays."

"Olive, your sanity is more important than tummy tucks, nose jobs, and all that other nonsense. People need to be happy with what nature gave them."

"Shh," I said, putting my fingertip to my lips. "Don't say that too loud. I might have to go out of business."

We both laughed.

"Listen, baby," I said, getting up from the table. "Why don't I go get the car while you pay the bill? Sometimes the valet can take forever."

"Won't you be too cold out there?" Hakim asked.

"No, I have a heavy overcoat." I quickly grabbed my coat. "See you in a few." I pulled my wool scarf over my head in an attempt to hide my face.

"Okay, baby," Hakim said. He grabbed my hand. "I can't wait to get you home so we can do it the right way."

I leaned in to him and whispered in his ear, "I really missed you, and when we get to my place, I'm going to show you just how much."

As I waited for the valet to bring the car around, I hoped I had made a clean getaway. Then I heard the dreaded words.

"Cynda? Is that you?"

I turned toward the voice. "Drayton, what are you doing here?"

"Just hanging out with a couple of friends. They're in town from New York."

"Cool," I said, nervously eyeing the front door of the restaurant.

"We were chilling at the bar when I spotted you walking out. Want to meet them?" he asked.

"I can't. I'm here on a date."

"A date?" He smirked. "You never have time to go on dates with me."

"You never ask."

"Maybe if I had a phone number or some way to contact you, I could."

The situation was not going well. Hakim would emerge from the door any second.

"You don't have a coat on, Drayton. Why don't you just go back inside before you catch a death of cold?"

"In other words, you don't want your man to run into me." He busted me.

"Basically."

Drayton rolled his eyes. "Whatever, Cynda. Your girl's a better fuck than you are anyway."

He leered at me a few seconds and then yanked the front door of the restaurant open just as Hakim was coming out. He looked back at me with disgust and then at Hakim. "Man, if that's you right there, you better watch out. She ain't shit!"

Hakim said, "What the fuck did you say?" He tried to go back into the restaurant but I grabbed him by the elbow. "What the fuck did he just say to me?"

"Don't worry about it, baby. He's just some drunken fool that followed me out from the bar, assuming I would give him some play. I told him that I was here with my man. My husband, in fact."

"Husband?" Hakim's entire demeanor changed. "I like the sound of that."

I kissed him on the cheek. "Then maybe that's something we should discuss, after we make love all night."

The valet finally pulled the car around. I let Hakim drive, even though we were only minutes away from my place. I was going to miss Drayton but it was just as well. All good things, including good fucks, must come to an end. Looking back, I realized I had let it go too far anyway. I was doing him too often, it was too much like being in a relationship. PID can be a mother-fucker. I had to keep in mind that I still had APF to satisfy my sexual urges. Yes, and there was Heaven. Fuck Drayton, I'd be all right.

I was a bit concerned about Mary Ann possibly telling my business. While I didn't think she was the type to run her mouth, she did have that Trevor idiot in her life. I had to hope that she wouldn't confide in him. Drayton had driven the knife kind of hard in me with that "your girl's a better fuck than you are anyway" comment. No one, even that country bumpkin, could outfuck me on my worst day.

patricia

I told Olive that I had to go back to the dorm to study. She knew me better than that but I didn't want to jinx my new rela-tionship. I couldn't even believe I was in one. It had happened so quickly.

I had been going through an automatic car wash two weeks prior when I spotted him through the rags that were pounding on my car. He was one of the men that finished off the car once the wash was complete. As a little girl, I used to love going through those car washes with my parents. It was almost like taking an amusement park ride, even though it only lasted a few minutes.

As an adult, I had grown accustomed to going through them and playing with my clit while I was in the car alone. I would put on some soft R & B music and play with myself, often coming before the car was finished. That's exactly what I was doing when I first saw him: playing with my clit.

The first thing I spotted were his luscious lips. His butter pecan complexion and thick eyebrows caught my attention. His slicked-back hair was like black silk. I wasn't sure of his nationality and I didn't care. All I knew was that I planned to fuck him.

Normally, I would stay in my car while the crew dried and waxed my car. This time, I got out. All of them were speaking Spanish to each other. I couldn't understand a word. Some things are universal, though, and I knew they were all checking me out and making remarks about my tits and ass. I had on a tight pair of jeans and a low-cut sweater. It was cold as shit outside too, but I didn't care. I was trying to figure out how I could seduce his ass if we didn't speak the same language. Then I realized this was America and all of them had to speak some kind of English, even if it was limited.

I looked him straight in the eye. "You speak English?"

He laughed at me. "Just as well as you do," he replied. "My buddies and I just prefer Spanish on the job."

"So you can talk about people without them knowing what you're saying?" I asked jokingly.

"Something like that."

"Hmm, but you do have an accent. A sexy one at that."

He blushed and showed a set of dimples I didn't know existed. "You think my accent is sexy?"

"Yeah, where's it from?"

"I'm Puerto Rican but I've been in the States more than ten years."

"Are you new here? I've never seen you and I get my car washed here a lot."

He shrugged his shoulders and looked up to his right like he was deep in thought. "I've been here about two months but I just went on full-time. It's hard getting a gig because the tips are really good."

I pulled him away from the other men while they finished up my car. I could tell they were trying to hear every word I was saying.

He was about the same height as me, shorter than I liked, but his fineness made up for it.

"Let me ask you this. Has anyone ever tipped you with pussy?"

"Now that would definitely be a first."

I grabbed the collar of his work overalls. "What's your name?"

"Alejandro."

"Nice name."

"Thanks. Do you have one?"

"Patricia. Patricia Reynolds." I clamped my eyes shut and said, "Fuck!"

He chuckled. "Your name is Patricia Reynolds Fuck?"

"No, just Patricia Reynolds."

I couldn't believe that I'd told him my real name. Not only my real first name but my real last name too. I was slipping.

Looking back on it now, I think that might have been a sign. A sign that I was ready to enter into an authentic relationship again. It had been a while since I'd been in one. I was seeing this dude named Maurice but he soon moved away.

After Alejandro got off work, I met him for dinner. He had been married, he told me. But his ex-wife, Manda, had decided to return home to Puerto Rico. She missed her parents and siblings too much to stay in America. He, on the other hand, had no intention of ever moving back there. Alejandro had goals and something about his character made me think he would have the determination to achieve them. I never thought I'd hook up with a car wash worker but as it turned out he did make pretty decent tips. He had a nice place in Langley Park, Maryland, and lived alone.

Amazingly, after talking much junk, I didn't even sleep with him that first night. He wouldn't allow it. He insisted on getting to know me better. At first, I wondered if he was gay. Not many men will turn down pussy. Especially, free easy pussy.

We did sleep together a few days later and it was the shit. He whispered to me in Spanish while we were going down on each other. I had no idea what he was saying but I knew it sounded sexy as hell. Yvette used to date this French dude and he would whisper sweet nothings to her in French. She would often brag about it but I wasn't feeling it. Now that I was banging Alejandro, I was definitely feeling it and then some.

That night, instead of studying like I'd told Olive, I was going to hang out with Alejandro at a Latin nightclub. He had promised to teach me how to do the "forbidden dance." There was a popular movie out at the time that I'd caught at a matinee where the people were competing doing the Lambada. It looked like they were fucking on the dance floor. In fact, I fucked the two dudes sitting three seats down from me in the theater for the hell of it. I told them my name was Sharisa.

We met and he drove us to the Latin Palace in Baltimore. I had heard a lot of ads for the place on the radio but figured all the hype about it was an exaggeration. That is, until I actually got there. It was awesome and crowded. The decor made me feel like I was on some island. And everyone in the place was shaking what their momma gave them.

Alejandro wasted no time taking me to the middle of the dance floor and wearing my ass out. I thought I was good at grinding but he taught me something new that night. An hour into it, I felt like I'd just had a gruesome workout at the gym. In fact, I told myself that I needed to start hitting the gym again on a regular basis.

I had on this tight black sheath and stiletto ankle boots, which made me slightly taller than him. We ordered a couple of frozen banana daiquiris and grabbed two stools in a dark corner. I gave him a hand job in the dark shadows while he fingered me. Then he let me lick myself off his fingers. Damn, that daiquiri sure made my pussy taste sweet!

We walked along the Baltimore harbor till about 1 A.M. and then crept onto an empty yacht and fucked up against the helm. Then we spent the night on the deck, covered by a wool throw. The next morning the owner ran us off, threatening to call the police. We laughed all the way back to the car.

21

mary ann

"Make yourself at home, Max," he said, turning on a torchère lamp in the living room of his apartment.

His name was Lucas and he was forty-nine. I thought as much. I was right on the money. He was an accountant for a large technology corporation. He lived alone on the Southwest waterfront in a high-rise adjacent to a marina. He claimed to have a boat that he promised to show me one day somewhere down there. I knew that that would never happen because I never planned to see him again beyond that night.

I wanted to know now what it would feel like to have sex with strangers on a regular basis, as would be the case if I joined APF. I wasn't sure I had it in me to do such a thing, but the way Olive and Patricia had described it had sounded so sensual and arousing. Then there was my experience that night at Heaven. Well, that had changed me. And then, there was Drayton. What a difference a few months can make in a person's life. I would never be the same.

"So, you never told me what Max was short for?" Lucas asked while he fixed us a pitcher of martinis.

"Maxine," I replied, lying. "My father wanted a boy and once he got over the disappointment, he convinced my mother to call me Maxine. Max, for short."

"That's cool." He handed me a glass and we toasted. "Here's to a wonderful evening." We sipped and then he said, "It's getting rather late."

"Yes, it is late but I'm a night owl."

"Me too; especially on the weekends. No need to rush out of bed in the mornings."

"True."

"So tell me, Max. What do you do for a living?"

"Does it matter?" I asked, laughing nervously.

"No, not really. Just trying to make conversation. After all, I've already told you so much about me and I hardly know a thing about you. I even confided in you about my ex-wife's profession."

"Tell the truth. Did it ever once turn you on?"

"Did what turn me on?"

"The fact that she was sleeping with other men."

He cleared his throat. "Honestly?"

"Yes, honestly."

"Ninety-nine percent of the time when I think about it, I feel nothing but pure disgust. But the other one percent of the time, I must admit that I am curious."

"Curious about what?"

"About what she would look like doing it with someone else. I understand she's even played around with other women."

I slid my hand up and down his thigh. "Well, that intrigues most men."

We both chuckled.

"Yes, I guess it does. But the thought of her being with another man, doing the same things she did with me, did arouse me somewhat."

"Why is that?"

"Just human nature, I guess. Something different. Something new. Life is all about experiences and creating memories."

I put my glass on the coffee table and then took his to do the same. I stood up in front of him and straddled him on the sofa, unbuttoning my blouse. "Care to create some memories with me?"

He ran his fingertips over my breasts. "You're something else, Max."

"So are you. Can I ask you one last question?"

"Sure."

"Since you found out about your ex, have you been reluctant to pick up women?"

"You're quite the mind reader. You sure you're not a psychiatrist?"

"No, but I am good at certain kinds of therapy."

I removed my blouse and reached behind me to undo the clasps on my bra.

"Oh, really? What types of therapy?"

"My specialty is sexual therapy."

I slipped my tongue into his eager mouth and wrapped my arms around his neck. His kisses were deep and passionate. I had never kissed an older man but his experience was showing.

Lucas pushed me away suddenly. "Max, come clean with me. Why are you doing this? Really?"

I hesitated. I couldn't decide whether an honest answer would be better than a fabrication. Then again, I wasn't sure what the honest answer would be.

"Because I want to know what it's like," I finally replied.

"What what is like?" he asked.

"Picking up a stranger and being intimate with him. Giving myself to someone completely. Someone I hardly know."

"And you've never done this before?"

"Not without guidance," I said, thinking that Olive had either dared me or drawn me into my other recent experiences. "I wanted to know what it felt like to be the aggressor."

"In other words, you've been picked up by men before but never actually picked one up?"

"Something like that." I began to feel uncomfortable, like I might back out. "Listen, can we just stop talking? I'm here because I want to be but if you want me to leave, just say the word. I want this to be mutual."

"And it will be," Lucas said before initiating another kiss.

I had tensed up and he could tell. "Why don't I run you a bath? Run us a bath. That might help us relax but I definitely don't want you to leave. You might very well be the most fascinating woman I've ever met."

I blushed. "Now that is quite the compliment. Just from the

little bit I know about you, I can tell that you're used to power-
ful, intelligent women."

"You mean other than my ex-wife?"

We both laughed.

Lucas took me by the hand and led me to his master bedroom. "Come on, let's relax."

After a luxurious bath in his garden tub, Lucas laid me
down on his king-sized bed. He wasn't rough or too aggressive
and he definitely wasn't foul mouthed. It was much different
than with Drayton. Lucas's body was spectacular for any age
and his soft hands were magical.

He kissed every inch of my body and even licked my ass-
hole. I had always thought that would make me cringe but it
turned me on so much. He sucked on each one of my fingers
and toes and even licked my underarms. But the most awesome
thing he did to me that night was eat my pussy. He took me to
another universe. It was unreal, the way he made me climax
over and over again. I felt like a buffet meal and he took his time
devouring me, pausing to lick up and down the inside of my
thighs from time to time.

When Lucas stuck his index finger in my ass, I almost
freaked but then I realized it felt good. That was about the time
it dawned on me that I was supposed to be the aggressor and I
was anything but at that moment. If I was going to do this, I was
going to do it the way I planned.

"Um, Lucas," I said, pushing his head from my pussy. "It's
my turn."

I could hear him chuckling. "All right, if that's the way you
want it."

"I do."

He lay on his back beside me and rested his head on his palms. "Do with me as you wish."

"Where do you keep your ties?"

"Why? Do you want to borrow one?"

"No, I want to tie you up."

"Hmm, I don't know about that. You might rob me."

"Do I look like a thief? The only thing I'm interesting in stealing is your dick." I rubbed my hand up and down his shaft. "Which, I might add, is splendid."

"Splendid dick." He grinned. "That's a new one."

"So where do you keep them?"

"I have a tie rack in my closet," he said, pointing to his right.

I entered his massive walk-in closet and admired his taste in clothes. Everything was pricey and well kept. He had at least fifty ties, mostly silk, hanging on a rack. I chose four of the finest and went back into the bedroom.

"Have you ever surrendered yourself totally to a woman before?" I asked, climbing on top of him.

"No, never," he replied. "I must admit that I'm a bit nervous about this. It's a big risk."

"So why are you taking it?"

"Because I think you're worth it."

I grinned as I bound his hands to the posts at the head of the bed. I purposely didn't make them too tight. Then I bound his feet to the posts at the foot of the bed.

"Believe it or not, I don't have much experience when it comes to sex."

Lucas laughed. "I find that very hard to believe."

"Seriously. Until a few months ago, my experiences were very limited. To one man, in fact."

"Let me guess. The man who left you at the restaurant?"

"Yeah, he and I had been together for years. Until I moved to D.C., I had never been with anyone but him."

"I noticed your accent. Are you from Tennessee or Alabama? I've been trying to place it."

"You're right on the money," I lied. "I'm from Birmingham."

"Cool. I have family down there. Maybe you know them. Their names are—"

I cut him off, knowing good and damn well I had never heard of them because I'd never been there. "Forget about that. Let me finish what I was saying."

"Okay," Lucas said, squirming on the bed.

"I've always wondered what it would be like to be in control. To climb on top of a man and have my way with him. I've always been amazed by women that can ride dicks with ease."

"How many women have you seen ride them?"

"Not many. Mostly in films."

"Ah, so you're into pornos. That's a good sign. It's healthy." I glanced around his room. "Do you have any?"

"Top drawer of the bureau."

I went over to his dresser and opened the top drawer. Sure enough, he had quite a collection. I selected one entitled *Nothing but Black Ass* and popped it into the VCR he had connected to a large television in the corner.

Once the tape started, it showed a couple lying by a pool. The woman was sucking the man's dick. That's not what I wanted to see so I used the remote to fast-forward it. About ten minutes into the tape, they showed a woman with large breasts sitting on top of a greatly endowed man and riding him to death.

I put the tape back on normal speed and climbed onto Lucas, whose dick hadn't softened the entire time. "Now let me see if I can compete with her," I said seductively.

"The woman on the tape?"

"Yes."

He lifted his head off the bed so he could see the television better. He chuckled after a few seconds. "This should be interesting."

I rubbed my clit over the head of his dick until I was nice and moist and then I used one hand to balance myself and the other to guide him into my pussy. "Umm, how does that feel?" I asked him.

His eyes were closed as he licked his lips. "That feels incredible."

"Good," I said, taking him in entirely. I put my hands on his chest, just like the woman in the film, and started slowly moving up and down on him.

About two minutes later, I realized my mistake and climbed off him.

"What's wrong?" he asked, opening his eyes and allowing them to adjust to the light.

"I forgot to ask you to wear a condom."

"I'm glad you remembered." He turned his head toward his nightstand. "There's a box in there."

I got the box of condoms out, ripped open a packet and put one on him. Then I climbed back on. By that time, the woman in the film was going really fast so I had to play catch-up. I started riding Lucas just as fast. When she turned around to face the man's feet, I turned around. When she got on her feet and put her hands behind her like a wheelbarrow, I did the same thing. When she spun around on his dick, so did I. Now that was off the hook.

Before I was done with Lucas that night, he had passed out from exhaustion. I untied his hands but didn't wake him. I found a pen and pad on his kitchen counter and left him a note that said:

Lucas,

Thanks for entertaining me last night. More importantly, thanks for the ride. It was nice meeting you and maybe someday we'll run into each other again.

Until then,
Max

22

olive

     I called Mary Ann about 3 P.M. to see if she had made a decision about attending freak night. The time had arrived.

She seemed nervous as she talked to me on the hallway phone. I finally just told her that if she planned to come, she should catch up with Patricia before six because that was when she was rolling out.

Hakim was hanging around the house that day. A bit too much for me. We had talked about marriage the night before and I had the feeling that he had probably already ordered a ring. He had gone out that morning to "handle some business." He was hyped. I was, too, but I was hoping marriage would not mean that he would cut back on his business travels. Part of the reason we had lasted so long was the fact that absence really does make the heart grow fonder. I didn't know if I could deal with Hakim being around all the time.

He had mentioned the word *babies* and I freaked out. I made no bones about it. I was not birthing anything for at least another three years. No exceptions. I was not ready to give up my shape, my time, and my freedom just yet. My parents had me very young and I heard nothing but their regrets all my life. They fought like cats and dogs. That's one reason I hauled ass clear across the country as soon as possible. They had only stayed together for me. Now that I was gone, there was nothing to hold them together. I was hoping they'd just go ahead and get a divorce so they could both move on. Life is too short to live in hell.

"Baby, I bought us tickets for that new black play at the Warner tonight," Hakim blurted out as he watered my plants in a pair of blue fluffy slippers. "It starts at eight."

I was winding the cord back around the vacuum when his statement stopped me in my tracks. "I can't go to a play tonight. I have plans."

"Plans? Do you know how hard it is to get decent seats at the Warner for *anything*?"

"I realize that, Hakim, but you should have told me before now. I have plans to hook up with Patricia and some of the girls tonight. It's Yvette's birthday."

I knew he was about to start whining by the way he put down the watering can and placed his hands on his hips. "Yvette's birthday? I don't even know an Yvette."

"Well, I do. Believe it or not, Hakim, I do have a life when you're out of town. Yvette and I go back a ways. She goes to school with Patricia and she's in our investment club."

Hakim knew about the investment aspect of APF but he thought we called it Black Women Entrepreneurs. We were entrepreneurs. Entrepreneurs when it came to money and hellified sex action.

"Well, can't you reschedule?" he asked with disdain.

"I'm supposed to reschedule ten or more women? We've been planning this thing for Yvette for months and it would be selfish of me to back out."

"Where are you going?"

I hesitated, trying to think of an answer. "Just hanging out in Annapolis."

"They have places to hang out in Annapolis?"

"Yeah, some really nice places. You're in Hong Kong so much that you don't even know that a bunch of new places have opened up."

"I've heard about that new club in Northeast. That warehouse place."

"Hmph, you won't catch me up in there. They actually make you pay to sit down."

"Really?"

"Is that some siddity stuff or what?"

"How much do you have to pay to sit down?"

"Hundreds for a table, from what I hear. Sometimes thousands. That's on top of having to pay out the ass to even get in."

"Well, there's not that much clubbing in the world."

"Exactly."

"Back to the play, you're really not going?"

"I can't. Why don't you take Alex with you?"

"Alex? I'm not trying to go to a play with a man. Plays are a couple date."

"So, people might assume you all are gay." I laughed. "You both know you're real men so don't sweat it."

"That's not even funny, Olive." He came over and put his arms around my waist from behind, kissing my neck. "I really want to spend some time with you, not Alex."

"We do and we will spend time together." I turned to face him and started caressing his dick. "Umm, looks like somebody else is awake. I haven't had a thing to eat today. Can I feed off him?"

Hakim kissed me on the forehead. "You know what I love most about you?"

"What?"

"You always know the perfect things to say."

I got down on my knees and pulled his pants down. "I also know the perfect things to do."

I arrived at the fire station about seven. Patricia and I were in charge of freak night and I was hoping her ass would be on time. Ironically, she beat me there and she was not alone.

"Mary Ann, nice to see you," I said, giving her a hug.

"Nice to see you too."

"Don't I get a hug?" Patricia asked sarcastically.

"Hell no," I chided. "I might catch something fishy."

"Very, very cute."

We all laughed.

We were in the kitchen and I sat down beside Mary Ann at one of the bench-style tables. "I'm glad you decided to come."

"It was a difficult decision. I won't even lie about it."

"So what made you lean in this direction?"

"I had this experience last night."

An *experience?* I was hoping it wasn't another fuck session with Drayton, even though I was done with his ass.

I was about to ask for details when Patricia's nosy ass jumped in. "Don't keep us in suspense. What type of experience?"

Mary Ann giggled like a schoolgirl, a country schoolgirl. "Well, the first wild thing that happened was my ex-boyfriend from back home showed up at my dorm."

"Clarence?" Patricia asked. I had never heard of his ass. "He came to see you from South Dakota?"

"Yes, he drove all the way here."

"Did you fuck him?" I asked, wanting to get to the nitty-gritty.

She shook her head. "No, not him."

"Trevor?" Patricia asked with sarcasm. "What's going on with the two of you anyway?"

"I'm in limbo right now with Trevor. I'll deal with him later. I plan to go home for Christmas and do some serious soul-searching. About Trevor, about a lot of things."

"Things like APF?" I asked.

"Yes. Even though I'm here, I'm not sure I can go through with this on a regular basis. You two have to understand that this is not normal behavior for me. I grew up very sheltered and I'm confused."

I started feeling a bit guilty. Maybe I was pressuring her too much. "Mary Ann, you're welcome to stay and observe tonight but don't feel like you have to participate."

"No!" she exclaimed. "I want to participate. This is sort of a test for me. Just like last night."

"Back to last night," Patricia said. "What happened between you and Clarence?"

"We went out to eat and I told him that I was seeing someone else. I also told him that I had been with a few other men since I moved here, and he went off, calling me a whore and bitch, and said he was going to get laid at a booty club."

Patricia and I both fell out laughing. "You go, girl," we said in unison.

"Anyway, after he left me at the restaurant, I approached this older man at the bar."

"You did what?" I asked in shock. Mary Ann was really coming into her element.

"I picked him up, all by myself. I went back to his place with him."

"You fucked him?" I asked.

"It was wild. At first, he was the one catering to me. He bathed me, licked me all over, even my ass and toes, and then ate me out. Then I insisted on taking control."

"So what did you do?" Patricia asked.

"I tied him to his bed with silk ties, put in a porno flick, and climbed on top of him. I called myself having a dick-riding competition with the sister on the tape."

I laughed. "Who won?"

"I did," Mary Ann boasted. "I whipped her ass and his."

We all exchanged high fives.

"How did it feel? Taking control?" I asked.

"It was great."

"So you like riding dick, huh?"

"That position does something to me. I can't wait to do it again."

Patricia rubbed her shoulder. "Well, they'll be plenty of dicks here tonight to ride."

"That's it," I said. "I was wondering what we would call you but now I know. From this moment on, you will be the one known as Soror Ride Dick."

Mary Ann giggled. "Soror Ride Dick?"

"It fits you perfectly."

"It damn sure does," Patricia agreed. "That's you. Soror Ride Dick!"

We sat there for a few minutes. I don't know about Patricia and Mary Ann, but I was thinking that I had apparently created another masterpiece. A woman that was able to let go of all her inhibitions and realize that having sex was nothing. Anyone can have sex. Having great sex, free sex, was what life was truly about.

There was a knock at the side door, which brought us all back down to earth. The other sorors had arrived. They were all amazed as they came in the door.

"A fire station?" Soror Three Input asked. "This is off the damn hook!"

"This is going to be so much fun," Soror Cum Hard added. "How did you ladies hook this one up?"

Patricia slapped her on the ass. "Where there's a will, there's a way."

"So what time do the men arrive?" Soror Gadget asked. Her specialty was sex toys and there was nothing she couldn't get off on; even common household items.

"Nine o'clock," Patricia answered, glancing at her watch. "We better get ready."

I couldn't help but notice that all of them were staring at Mary Ann. A couple of them looked like they wanted to sneer at her but they knew better.

I pulled Mary Ann up off the bench, put my arm around her shoulder and announced, "Ladies, Soror Ride Dick is in the house!"

Soror Gadget was the first to hug her. "Soror Ride Dick! You're not fucking around, are you, sistergirl? That's a cool-ass name."

Over the next hour, they all loosened up around Mary Ann. Not that they had a choice. My rules were law, *period!*

mary ann

When the men arrived, I was loose and ready. All the sorors had been kind and I was tipsy from all the alcohol that had been passed around. Some of the sorors were smoking weed but that was one habit I was not trying to start. I was not there to judge them, though. After all, I was at a freak night for Alpha Phi Fuckem. If only my daddy could see me now.

I quickly got that thought out of my head though. In fact, I blocked everyone out but the people that were in the fire station. Trevor had come by my room earlier that day and I had brushed him off then. I wasn't ready to deal with him, and every time I looked at him, I thought about FeFe sucking his dick. I told him that I would call him when I got back from the holiday break and let him know where I'd be living.

The men came in together. They were all fine. Different heights, shapes, ages, sizes, but all fine. I took a deep breath as they took in the scene. Thirteen women standing there in nothing but firemen's coats, boots, and hats. Other than that, we were butt-ass naked.

All the sorors took turns introducing themselves. The men just stood there with their mouths hanging open. One man asked, "What on earth did I do to deserve this?"

I was the last to give an introduction and it felt weird and invigorating at the same time to mouth the words, "I'm Soror Ride Dick. Welcome."

As soon as the words left my lips, I knew I was in for it. Those men probably expected me to be the dick rider of all dick riders. I could tell. I was going to try my best to live up to it.

Olive broke out a box of assorted condoms; looked like thousands and informed them, "The sorors of Alpha Phi Fuckem only practice safe sex so don't get it twisted. If any of you want to play that 'I can't feel anything with a condom' routine, you need to get the fuck out now because we're not down for that nonsense. Some of you may be invited back; most of you won't be so you better make the most of tonight. This shit might not ever, ever happen to you again. We all like to fuck, pure and simple. No, scratch that. We love to fuck but we won't be fucked over. We are in control and you are our sex slaves for tonight. Any issues with that, get the fuck out."

None of the men said a word. They just stood there with their mouths hanging open.

Olive continued. "All of you brothers are looking mighty fine tonight and that's a good thing. But fineness only goes so far. We want to see some dick. Now strip!" That was the start of freak night and it was unbelievable. I took a position on top of one of the fire trucks, on a pile of hoses. The first two men I fucked were so-so. I had just had Lucas the night before and there was no comparison. The third man got so excited when I rode him that he took me by surprise, flipped me over, and almost broke my back. I didn't think he'd ever come.

I did nine men altogether that night. I am not sure how many Olive did but I think Patricia might very well have fucked all of them. Sorors had men spread out all over the station. In the barracks upstairs, in the kitchen, all over the trucks, and I saw Soror Gadget hanging upside down on one of the sliding poles getting fucked by two men; one in her pussy and one in her mouth.

When I got back to my dorm the next morning, I slept almost until sunset. Then I woke up and masturbated, thinking about freak night. While it was more than I could have dreamed, I still had some emotional issues I needed to deal with. If my parents ever found out, would they lose all respect for me? How could they ever find out, though, unless I told them? Even if they never found out, could I live with the guilt?

What on earth was I going to do about Trevor? Did he really love me or was I just a token? Could I somehow improve him in the bedroom? How serious did I really want to get with him? What would becoming a member of APF do to my law career? Could I continue to concentrate on my schoolwork if I was out fucking all the time?

I stared up at my ceiling. "Where on earth am I going to figure out all these answers?"

23

mary ann

I was so excited to be back home that I almost tumbled down the steps of the bus. I was too afraid to fly after all. Daddy was waiting for me right on the curb. I flung my arms around him and planted kisses all over his face.

"Calm down, Mary Ann," he said, laughing. "You're about to choke me to death."

I let go of him and just stared at his face. "I'm sorry, Daddy. I just missed you so much. You and everybody else."

"Well, then, let's hurry up and get your bags so we can get on home. Your mother is probably pacing the floor waiting for us to get back."

Luckily, my luggage was near the front of the baggage compartment underneath the bus. Within five minutes, we were in his truck and hitting the highway. It was twenty-two degrees and snow was still on the ground from the latest winter storm. Thank goodness I had been smart enough to put my snow boots in my bag.

"So how's school?" he asked.

"It's great, Daddy. I've met so many interesting people."

"I know you don't call like you used to." I could hear the disappointment in his voice. "It almost seemed like you deserted me."

"Aw, Daddy, you know that you will always be the number one man in my life." I rubbed him on the arm. "I've just been adjusting to my new surroundings."

He cleared his throat. "I heard Clarence drove up there to see you."

"Where did you hear that?"

"Please! As small as this town is, we hear when someone gets a speeding ticket. You know that."

I giggled. "True."

"Well, don't keep me in suspense. What happened when he came up there?"

"Nothing much. Actually, we had an argument and he left."

I could feel my dad take his eyes off the road for a minute to stare at me. "An argument about what? Don't tell me the two of you broke up after all this time?"

"Clarence and I broke up before I left town. I thought it would be for the best. There was no way we could continue a long-distance relationship, so we decided to just be close friends."

"And he went along with that?" Daddy asked suspiciously.

"I didn't really leave him a choice." I sighed. "Besides, he started dating Jessica Williams the second I left town."

"Really? Isn't Jessica the town tramp?"

"Hmph, I couldn't tell you." I could hear the jealousy in my own voice and I hated it. "It doesn't matter. She can have Clarence because . . ."

I hesitated. I hadn't even mentioned Trevor to either of my parents and I wasn't sure how they would react. After all, I had jumped into a relationship my first semester of law school.

I wasn't fooling Daddy though. "She can have Clarence because what?"

"I'll tell you later." I turned the radio up. "I just want to relax for a minute after that bus ride. I'm sure that seeing everyone is going to be overwhelming."

He snickered. "Yes, I'm sure it will be and you have a surprise waiting for you back at the farm."

"A surprise?"

"Uh-huh, a big surprise."

"Daddy, you didn't buy me a car, did you?"

"Naw, baby, I wish. Your mother and I really want to make that happen for you but we just can't afford it right now. Maybe next year."

I felt like crap. "It's okay. It was just a guess. I don't have anywhere to keep a car in D.C. anyway," I lied. Hartsdale had plenty of student parking. I just didn't want him to feel bad about it.

"Like I said, maybe next year."

He grew silent and I pulled down the visor so I could check myself out in the mirror. Mommy was likely to make comments about my appearance if something was out of place.

I shut the visor back. "So give me a hint about the surprise."

"I can tell you this. It's a *human* surprise."

"Aw, the plot thickens. You and Mommy haven't had another baby since I left town?"

"Not a chance. That bank is closed."

"So that means someone is visiting. I wonder who."

"And you'll continue wondering until we get home," he chided.

I pouted the rest of the way but underneath the facade, I was excited to see my family and to find out who the surprise was.

My three younger sisters were bundled up and waiting at the end of the long driveway by the mailbox when we pulled up. They were jumping up and down as Daddy stopped the truck so I could get out and hug them. Caroline, Liza, and Amelia all seemed like they had grown several inches since I had been gone but I know that was just my imagination. I was in tears when Liza screamed out in excitement that she had started her period the month before. She had traded her pigtails in for long, flowing curls. Caroline told me that Daddy was letting her operate the tractor, and Amelia was going out for the girls' softball team at the junior high. They were all going to be dating and driving by the time I got out of law school.

I waved Daddy on so that I could walk up the driveway with them. We played catch-up on the latest news. My cousin Lucille was pregnant with her fifth baby; the fifth one without the benefit of marriage. That was no big deal to me because she had been living with her boyfriend, Mathis, for almost twelve years. They also said that Daddy had taken to letting eggs incubate in our dishwasher again. That was disgusting but common in our household during the winter. Visitors would often lose their stomach contents when they found out. My brother Caleb loved to brag about it. Otherwise, it would have just remained our family secret.

When we got up to the house, Daddy already had my bags off the truck and Mommy was on the front porch waiting for us. She looked so gorgeous, and while I had managed to hold back tears to that point, I found myself breaking down. No matter how old a person gets, there is nothing more heartwarming than a motherly hug, and when she wrapped her arms around me, I was like a two-year-old again.

My four brothers came running from the back of the house, engaged in a snowball fight. They were so caught up in their little game that they didn't even notice me.

"Boys!" Daddy yelled. "Get your tails over here and welcome Mary Ann home!"

They dropped their snowballs just long enough to hug me. My father was raising them tough and, like my father, they didn't believe in showing a lot of affection.

I was overcome with emotion but the "surprise visitor" was still weighing heavily on my mind.

"Mommy, who's the visitor?" I asked.

Mommy just giggled, along with the girls, and said, "Come on in the house. See for yourself."

I walked into the living room and threw my hands over my mouth when I spotted my Aunt Venus standing in the middle of the floor.

"Aunt Venus!" I exclaimed, running to her and sharing an embrace. "It's been so long!"

"Mary Ann, look at you," she said, moving slightly away from me and checking me out. "God, you have grown."

"It's been at least eight years since I've seen you."

"Nine, to be exact."

Aunt Venus is my father's twin sister. She moved away to Chicago right after high school, saying that she couldn't live in a "backass" town for one more day. Of all my relatives, I had always admired her the most. She took the bull by the horns, made her own decisions, and controlled her own life.

She had attended the University of Chicago on scholarship for undergrad and medical school and had a flourishing private practice. I was so proud of her. I couldn't wait to pick her brain about many things, but first I wanted to see what they had done to my room.

I was startled to find my room exactly the way I had left it. With the exception of my television being missing, everything was in place. I was sitting on my window seat looking out over the horizon when Mommy appeared in the doorway.

"I know you thought this would be a totally different room by now."

"I did. Don't you all need the space?"

"Eventually, but I just couldn't see breaking down your room the second you walked out the door." She came to sit beside me. "It's not easy letting go."

I laughed. "Tell me about it. It's so hard for me to be there while all of you are here. I feel like I'm missing something every day. The kids all look five years older, even though it has only been a few months."

"That's the thing about kids. One day you're birthing them and the next day they're going off to law school." She rubbed my thigh. "You want to take a nap before dinner? You must be exhausted."

"Actually, I feel fine but I could use a bath. That bus trip made me feel so dirty."

"Then I'll go run the water," Mommy said as she stood up.

"You don't have to do that. I'm perfectly capable."

She leaned over and kissed me on the forehead. "Let me be a mother. Don't deprive me of this moment."

Daddy had placed my luggage on the bed, so I found something to put on. A framed picture of Clarence was still on my nightstand. I tossed it in the trash.

After my bath, I joined everyone for dinner and the conversation was lively. I could barely get a word in. By the time someone asked me something, someone else was asking me something else, before I could answer.

Aunt Venus was bombarded with questions as well. Tall and gorgeous, she's always looked more like a supermodel than a doctor. So the boys in particular asked her if she knew anyone famous. She said she knew a few people but only in passing. They seemed bored and moved on to the next series of questions.

It was two days until Christmas and I was disappointed that I had missed the tree-trimming, which is always a major event in the Ferguson household. Daddy and the boys went deep into the woods to select the perfect tree while Mommy, the girls, and I would always decorate with homemade ornaments. We had made at least ten new ones yearly so the tree had to get bigger and bigger. The one they had in the corner of the living room this year was huge and still seemed overcrowded with decorations. The ceramic angel I had made in the fourth grade was in its righteous place on the top of the tree.

We stayed up late into the night, drinking eggnog and making apple cobblers. Mommy always donated some to the church bake sale every year. Daddy passed out with the kids around midnight while Mommy, Aunt Venus, and I sat at the kitchen table playing catch-up.

Mommy finally asked the dreaded question. "How are things with Clarence?"

I gauged her expression and smirked. "Mommy, I can tell by the look on your face that Daddy told you Clarence and I broke up."

She picked up another apple to peel. "He might have mentioned it."

Aunt Venus asked, "Isn't that the young man you've been seeing for a long time?"

"Yeah," I replied. "Since high school."

"So what happened?" Mommy inquired. "I assumed the two of you would get hitched one day."

I giggled. "*Hitched* is such an ugly word. To make a long story short, Clarence and I both started seeing other people."

"Which means you're seeing someone else?" Mommy asked.

"Yes. His name is Trevor. Trevor Ames."

"You met him in D.C."

I nodded. "He goes to Hartsdale with me." I decided to get all the major data out in the open. "He's in his third year, top of the class, six and a half feet tall, handsome, originally from Gary, Indiana. He has his own place and he drives a Porsche."

Aunt Venus snickered. "Damn, I need to hook up with him."

Mommy looked concerned. "Are you sleeping with him?"

"Mom! I'm grown and I have no problem saying that I am." That was a bold move for me. The old me would have denied it. "In fact, Trevor has asked me to move in with him next semester."

Mommy stood up and walked over to the sink to wash a colander of apple slices. "Don't tell me you plan to do it?"

"Honestly, I'm not sure. I'm considering it."

She sat back down at the table. "Listen, Mary Ann, you know I've never tried to tell you what to do. I was happy when you decided to leave the state and follow your dream by attending Hartsdale, but you shouldn't tie yourself down so quickly."

"A second ago you were talking about Clarence and me getting hitched."

"I know, and your relationship with Clarence never really set right with me either. It was just something I accepted. But now that the two of you broke up, you don't need to jump right into something serious with someone else."

"I agree," Aunt Venus said. "Especially in a city like D.C. There are so many men there. You need to take your time and make the right choices."

"D.C. might have a lot of men but it also has a lot of women competing for the attention of the few available men." I stared at my mother. "Mommy, are you actually telling me that I should play the field?"

"All I'm saying is you need to enjoy life and not make any hasty decisions. I love your daddy. God knows I do, but he's the only man I've ever been with. My family thought I was crazy, but, I would never take a day of it back. However, there have been times when I wondered what would have happened if I had gotten away when I was younger for even a little while. I know that my heart would have led me back to him. There is no doubt. But it would have been nice to experience other things before we settled down. I'm sure if you asked him, he'd say the same thing."

"Mary Ann, look at me," Aunt Venus said. "I've never married but I'm having the time of my life. I date on a regular basis but I see no reason to tie myself down to one man. Times are changing."

I don't know what made me do it. Maybe it was my desperate search for answers. Maybe it was just pure stupidity. Whatever it was, before I knew it, I was beating around the bush about Alpha Phi Fuckem.

"There's this group of women who asked me to join them," I said. "They have this investment club and—"

"That's great, baby." Mommy tapped me lightly on the hand. "Every woman needs to save her money. The cost of living is ridiculous these days."

"True, but they also do other things."

"Other things like what?"

"Um, they have these special nights where they invite men to—"

"Oh my goodness!" Aunt Venus jumped back and screamed out. "I cut my finger!"

She had a deep gash on her index finger from a paring knife. Mommy jumped up to get some hydrogen peroxide and a bandage. I helped Aunt Venus into the guest bathroom to wash the blood away.

She looked at my reflection in the mirror. "Mary Ann, go to bed."

"Huh?"

"I said go to bed."

I was confused. "But why? We were talking and—"

She turned to face me. "Just do as I say and don't say another word about the group you mentioned. Tell your mother that you're tired and will see her in the morning."

"But Aunt Venus—"

She grabbed my wrist. "Alpha Phi Fuckem is a top-secret sorority, as I'm sure you already know. You're dead wrong for even hinting about it."

"How do you know about APF?"

We heard Mommy coming toward the bathroom. "I have the bandage."

"Good night, Mary Ann," Aunt Venus mumbled.

I did what I was told. I lied to Mommy and said I was too tired to keep my eyes open, and went upstairs. I didn't sleep a wink that night though. Not one single wink.

24

patricia

Alejandro and I did our last-minute Christmas shopping together. I still had not mentioned him to a soul. I felt like I might jinx our relationship if I did. Things were going too perfectly and that meant almost too good to be true. I was not taking any chances.

I did allow him to carry some bags up to my dorm room. It was safe because the majority of people were out of town for the winter break. There I made love to him in my bed for the first time. There is nothing more comfortable than doing it in your own bed.

Afterward, I asked, "Do you want to go out for dinner?"

He kissed my shoulder and spooned me. "Actually, I was thinking we could go back to my place so I could cook for you."

I sat up on my elbows. "You cook?"

"Shit, I'm one hell of a cook. In Puerto Rico, I was cooking complete dinners by the time I was eight. My parents worked all day and night."

"What do they call Puerto Rican food? Is there a name for it?"

"Locals call it *cocina criolla*."

"Cocina criolla?"

"Yeah. Puerto Rican food is a mixture of African, Spanish, Taino, and American."

"So what is your specialty?"

"Jeez, I have so many of them. Hmm, let's see. I make the empanadillas."

"What are those?"

"They're little turnovers filled with different meats and spices."

"Cool."

He ran his fingers through my hair. "Well? Are you going to let me cook for you?"

"Sure," I replied, turning to face him and climbing on top. "As soon as you give me some more of that Puerto Rican salami."

We got back to his place about nine that night, after stopping at a small grocery store that carried everything he would need to do his thing.

I watched him rush around the kitchen diligently preparing several dishes: *frijoles negros* (black bean soup), fried green plantains, *arroz con pollo* (chicken with rice), *camarones en cerveza* (shrimp with beer), and *boudin de pasas con coco* (coconut bread pudding).

I felt like a stuffed pig after I finished eating at least two servings of everything. It was so delicious.

I helped him clean up. That was the least I could do. Then we curled up in front of his television and watched some Spanish films. It was weird. The films didn't have subtitles and even though I didn't have a clue what they were saying, I still found myself caught up in the drama. A few times I asked Alejandro what something meant but, for the most part, I just lived with it. One film about a young girl who commits suicide over a lost love had me in tears.

"You all right, baby?" he asked, cradling me in his arms.

"I'll be just fine," I managed to say between sniffles. "This is just too sad."

"Maybe I can cheer you up."

Alejandro got up and went into the kitchen. I was hoping he wasn't about to break out anything else to eat. He returned a minute later with a sliced mango on a plate.

"Baby, I don't think I can eat another thing."

"Oh, this isn't for you to eat." He grinned. "This is for me to eat off you."

"Um, now that sounds interesting."

"It will be," he said.

olive

Hakim got to my place a little after eleven. It was about damn time because my PID was kicking in like a motherfucker. If he hadn't gotten there soon, I was likely to be tempted to go pick up some dick.

I had calmed down a lot from the old me. That shit I was engaged in with Drayton was just ridiculous. Hit-and-run fucks would have to suffice from now on; no matter how good the dick was.

I had ordered Italian food to be delivered. It arrived cold, so I heated up the lasagna and garlic bread for Hakim while he grabbed a quick shower. Afterward, I sat on his lap at the dining room table and fed him. He just loved that shit. So did I.

I enjoyed babying him. Hakim was such a breast man that I would often sit on the couch and breast-feed him for hours. Thank goodness my breasts were not sagging but I was prepared if they ever did. One of the many benefits of being a plastic surgeon was that I knew just the person to do the honors if it ever came down to pulling my tits back up into place. The good doctor and I went to medical school together.

After dinner, Hakim and I grabbed a couple of beers and sat down in front of my gas fireplace.

"Olive, I've been thinking."

"About what, baby?"

"Us."

I lifted his hand and kissed his palm. "I think about us all the time too."

"Do you really?"

He glared at me through the firelight.

"You look so serious. What's wrong?"

"Nothing's wrong. In fact, everything's right. Nothing has ever felt so right. At least, not for me. I just want to make sure you feel the same way."

"I do."

"Say that again."

"Say what again?" I asked.

"What you just said."

"I do?"

"Yeah, that. Sounds like a symphony." He reached behind his back and pulled out a black velvet box. "Care to say it again, say, nine to twelve months from now?"

I gasped. I knew the day would come but I wasn't expecting it right that second. "What did you do, Hakim?"

"Something I should have done a long time ago." He placed the box in my hand. "Open it. Consider it an early Christmas present."

I opened the box to discover a four-carat solitaire set in a platinum band. "Hakim, it's exquisite."

"Not as exquisite as you, Olive. From the first moment I saw you, I knew that I'd marry you one day. It was always just a matter of time."

"I'm at a loss for words."

"Allow me to help you out." Hakim took the ring out of the box and placed it on my ring finger. "Try saying yes."

The ring was heavy. It must have cost a mint. I just stared at it, running all types of scenarios through my mind.

"Well? Is it a yes or a no, Olive?"

"It's a yes!"

We tongued each other down, then got naked in the middle of the floor and made love. Hakim had never before filled me with such passion. For a brief moment, I contemplated giving up APF. After all, I was about to become a married woman. Then I thought about all the freak nights, all the fun, all the camaraderie amongst the sorors. Fuck no! APF till the day I die!

25

mary ann

Aunt Venus and I were finishing up two plates of the country-fried steak special at the local diner called Spoons. We'd been quiet for most of the meal. I looked out the window, taking in the scenery. People were rushing up and down the main street in town, getting the last-minute things they needed for Christmas Day. Christmas Eve is hectic, even in small towns.

"I'm glad you decided to join me for lunch today," she finally said.

"Are you kidding? I couldn't sleep last night after what you said to me."

She placed her napkin on the table and folded her hands in front of her. "I imagine you couldn't. I guess I should explain."

"That would be nice. How did you know I was talking about APF?"

"Now that should be obvious."

"You're a member."

"I'm more than that." She eyed the older couple at the table next to us. They were lost in their own conversation. "I'm a founding member of Alpha Phi Fuckem."

"You're kidding."

"Do I look like I'm kidding?"

"Aunt Venus, this is unbelievable."

She laughed. "Why is it unbelievable? I'm a sexually vibrant woman, just like the rest of the sorors. I have needs and desires that I choose to fulfill in an unusual way."

"So how long have you been a member?"

"Since the very beginning, like I said. I was one of the people that originally came up with the idea and the name."

I was confused. Aunt Venus had gone from South Dakota straight to Chicago. "But you never lived in D.C. I thought it was founded in D.C."

"It was founded there, you're right. And I never actually lived there. One of my best friends from the University of Chicago was from there. I used to go home with her for all the holidays instead of coming back to this piece of nowhere."

I grew anxious to know everything. "This is crazy. Why did you decide to do it? How many of you started it? Does Daddy know?"

"Slow down with the questions. Hell no, your father doesn't know. As far as I'm concerned, he never will. That's the whole point. APF members are the only people that know the real deal."

Our waiter came over. I had been staring at him during the entire lunch, thinking I may have gone to high school with him, but I didn't recognize the name on his badge. "Can I get you ladies something else?"

"Just some more iced tea, please," Aunt Venus said.

"I'll take some also," I said. There's nothing like sweetened iced tea and it was practically nonexistent in the D.C. area.

He said, "Be right back."

After he walked away, she continued. "It was the seventies and sisters were getting wild and freaky when it came to sex. But most of them were doing it without considering the consequences. They didn't care who knew what they were doing and were open about their promiscuity. Not us. We decided early on that we had too much to lose."

"So you started APF?"

"Yes. It took us about a year to plan the entire thing. There were nine of us. Two of us have passed on but the remaining seven are still members. One of the founding members is a senator."

"Get out of town!"

"I'm serious. You'll meet her, if you become a member. I assume from the way you were talking last night that you're undecided."

"Yes, I am." The waiter returned with a pitcher of tea and refreshed our glasses. I waited until he was out of earshot. "I feel guilty."

Aunt Venus shook her head. "Guilty about what? The man you're seeing?"

"Not really. I feel guiltier about Mommy and Daddy. What would they ever think?"

"They'll never know." Aunt Venus reached across the table and took my hand. "I have to say this. Unless you're absolutely sure that this is what you want, you shouldn't join APF. Walk away."

I lowered my eyes to the table in shame. "Aunt Venus, since I've been in D.C., I've done some things. Things I never thought I would do in a million years. I even attended a freak night."

"And how did it feel?"

"Different. Good." She tightened her grip on my hand. I looked at her and grinned. "Great!"

She snickered and took a large sip of her tea. "I'm curious. How did you get mixed up with APF in the first place?"

I hesitated for a few seconds but then realized that founding members probably knew more about the sorority, including the membership, than anybody. "My resident monitor is a member. She introduced me to the head of the D.C. chapter and then the two of them asked me to join."

"Aw, so you know Olive. Is she still using that ridiculous Olive Cox name when she is avoiding people?"

We both giggled.

"Yes. I wasn't buying that name from the beginning. Who in their right mind would name a child that?"

Aunt Venus let go of my hand but leaned in closer. "Olive is a wild girl but she's also very smart. I know her well. She wouldn't have asked you to join unless she felt you could handle it."

I thought about what happened with Drayton and at Heaven. "Looking back at it, I realize she put me through a series of tests."

"What kind of tests?" Aunt Venus asked. Then waved her hand and said, "Never mind. I can imagine."

Suddenly there was a banging on the window. Clarence was standing there with fire in his eyes. "Hey, bitch!" he spewed at me. Some of his saliva hit the pane.

He stomped off down the street.

"Who on earth was that?" Aunt Venus asked.

I rolled my eyes toward the ceiling. "That would be Clarence. He's really bitter toward me right now."

"I can see that. He better be glad he ran away so fast or I would have gone out there and crammed my foot up his ass."

I laughed. "Aunt Venus, you are a mess." I spotted Clarence walking across the street at the corner. He wasn't looking and almost got hit by a milk truck. Stupid fool. I couldn't imagine what I'd ever seen in his sorry ass.

"Mary Ann, search your soul for the answer. I wouldn't have done this for all these years unless I felt it was right for me. Only you can decide what's right for you."

"But is it fair for me to be in a relationship, possibly even a marriage, and still participate in APF?"

"We've all done it, baby. What a person doesn't know can't hurt them." Aunt Venus finished up her tea and I took a few sips of mine. That country-fried steak had filled me up and I was afraid to drink too much more. "The fact is there are good men who are perfect in every way except for one. A lot of men simply don't know how to treat a woman right sexually and a lot of the ones who do are seriously lacking in other departments."

I nodded in agreement. "That's the problem with Trevor, but you can't tell him that he's not the ultimate in the bedroom."

"Then it's up to you to make him the man you want him to be. Only if he's worth the aggravation."

That was a deep statement. Was Trevor worth it? I'd have to face him when I returned to D.C., and from the way he was talking it was either all or nothing. There was no in between.

"Is he?" she asked.

"Good question." I glanced at my watch. "We better get back before people start worrying."

"I hope this conversation has helped you." Aunt Venus laid two twenties on the table and got up to follow me out of the restaurant. "Just promise me one thing."

"What's that?"

"If you decide to join APF, let me know immediately. I'd like to attend your ceremony."

I was stunned. "Ceremony?"

"Yes, every soror is officially inducted into APF with a ritual. It's quite exciting too."

"Well, I'll be sure to let you know."

26

patricia

The second of January and I was still recovering from my New Year's Eve hangover. Alejandro and I had really lived it up at the Baja Club in Baltimore. I must have had at least a dozen glasses of champagne and several gin and tonics to boot. I had a migraine that wouldn't quit and I felt like my head was about to explode, especially when somebody started banging on my door.

"Patricia!" she screamed. "Patricia! Open up! It's me, Mary Ann!"

"Now what are the fucking odds of me not knowing your voice!" I screamed back at her, pulling the pillow over my head.

"Patricia, I need to talk to you!"

"Shit!" I managed to get up and stumble across the floor. "What is the damn emergency?" I asked as I flung the door open.

Mary Ann was standing there in all her glory, grinning like a schoolgirl. "Aren't you glad to see me? I just got back."

She barged her way into the room and sat down in my desk chair.

"Um, I'll be glad to see you tomorrow. Right now, my head is freakin' killing me."

"Too much to drink?" she asked.

I climbed back in the bed and put the pillow over my head, mumbling, "You're such a genius, Mary Ann."

"Patricia, there's no easy way to say this so I'll just blurt it out. I came to a decision about APF."

Now *that* got my attention. "You did?" I asked, sitting straight up. "What is it?"

"I really want to tell you and Olive at the same time. You think she's around?"

"She should be. I'm sure I can conjure her ass up."

"Then do that." Mary Ann got up and headed to the door. "I haven't even unpacked yet so give me thirty minutes to get settled, grab a shower, and get dressed."

olive

I was at the office lining up my first twenty or so patients for the year when my receptionist told me Patricia was on the phone. I picked it up and started going off on her before she could even say hello. "Patricia, you know good and damn well this is one of my biggest days of the year. A bunch of the hoes have already been flying in here all morning, happy as shit that their men have agreed to pay for them to 'get beautiful' for their Christmas gifts. I bet mad pussy was exchanged this holiday season."

"Olive, shut the hell up and listen," she snarled.

"Girl, you better slow your roll. I may be happy but I'm not the one to talk to like that. Not today, not ever."

"Whatever, slut! Mary Ann and I need to see you."

"Today?"

"In a little bit."

"But I'm busy," I declared. "I can hook up with you all later tonight. Bet?"

"Bet nothing. Mary Ann said she made up her mind about APF, but she won't tell me without telling you so we're on our way over there."

That changed things for me. I was dying to know what the country bumpkin had decided. "How soon can you be here?"

"See you within the hour."

Patricia hung up and I sat back in my chair and grinned. "I have faith in my girl. She's going to join."

Like clockwork, the three of us were standing together exactly an hour later. I chose examination room four to talk because it was at the end of the hall and more private than my office.

"Well, don't keep us in suspense any longer," I said.

"Okay," Mary Ann replied. "This was not an easy decision."

"It seldom is," Patricia said. "Alpha Phi Fuckem is a very serious matter and one that shouldn't be taken lightly."

Mary Ann nodded. "I agree. A very wise person schooled me on APF while I was in South Dakota."

Patricia and I glared at each other. "South Dakota!" I exclaimed. "What the fuck are you talking about?"

"Calm down." Mary Ann giggled. "I have something shocking to tell you."

"Which is?"

"Olive, do you happen to know someone named Venus?"

It couldn't be! "Yeah, I know a Venus. The question is how do you know her?"

"My *Aunt* Venus."

"Your what?" Patricia inquired. "Let me get this straight. The Venus in question, which could only be the same Venus, is your aunt?"

"My father's twin sister, to be exact. She was home visiting from Chicago. We had lunch on Christmas Eve and one thing led to another."

"Who brought up APF?" I asked suspiciously.

"Does it matter?" Mary Ann replied. "All that matters is that Aunt Venus connected the dots. Then she explained the history of APF to me, what it's really all about, and what I could realistically hope to gain from it."

Patricia walked around the table and placed her hand on top of Mary Ann's. "Are you saying what I think you're saying, Mary Ann?"

She grinned. "Mary Ann. Who's that? I'm Soror Ride Dick!"

Patricia hugged Mary Ann while I shook my head and said, "I knew you had it in you. It's strange how some things come about. But, everything happens for a reason. Old Venus. Damn!

I never would have seen this one coming. Are you telling me that Venus is originally a country bumpkin from South Dakota like your ass?"

Mary Ann laughed. "Amazing, isn't it? You'd never be able to tell from the way she is now."

"Fucking tell me about it!" I exclaimed. "Venus is one of the most sophisticated sisters I've ever met in my entire life."

"Me too," Patricia agreed.

"So, what's next?" Mary Ann asked.

I went over to her and kissed her once on each cheek. "Next comes your official induction. Let's pick a date."

"Wow, I feel like I'm getting married," Mary Ann said jokingly.

I slapped myself on the forehead. "I almost forgot. I am getting married. Hakim proposed." I flashed my ring.

"Damn!" Patricia said. "I'm surprised we weren't both blinded when we walked in the room."

I giggled. "You're fucking silly!"

"Congrats, Olive!" Mary Ann said.

Patricia embraced me. "Yes, congrats, soror! And you better have my ass in your wedding!"

"I plan to have both of you in my wedding!"

Mary Ann giggled and said, "Then that means we have two dates to pick."

27

mary ann

It was time for me to lay down the law. My decision to join APF finalized some things in my mind. Mainly, I wasn't going to just settle for anything when it came to sex. Not even with Trevor.

When we left Olive's office, I asked Patricia to drop me off at Trevor's house. He hadn't gone home to Indiana for the holidays and his car was in his spot when we pulled up. I thought to myself that if FeFe or some other bitch was in there sucking his dick, I was going to have to hurt somebody.

Trevor answered the door as soon as I rang the bell. He had on a wool overcoat and gloves.

"Oh, were you on your way out?"

"Baby!" He grabbed me up into his arms. "I was about to go to the bar down the street and grab a few beers. I'm not going anywhere now that you're here."

He carried me inside and put me down on the sofa.

"Wow, you must be really glad to see me," I said.

"You have no idea. Why didn't you call me to pick you up at the bus station? I still say you should have let me pay for you to fly home."

"I'm leery of flying. You know that."

"But that's a long-ass ride." He took his gloves off and took my hands into his. "You're too precious a cargo to be on an un-comfortable-ass bus that long."

"You're so sweet." I pulled my hands away. "Trevor, we really need to talk."

"I hope we're about to talk about the easiest way to get you moved in here."

"Possibly, but we need to straighten some things out first."

"Some things like what?" He stood up to take his coat off. "Let me help you with your coat."

"I can handle it." After I wriggled out of my coat, I said, "I really adore you, Trevor, even though we've had our ups and downs. Some things are just instilled in you, like being a playa, but I'm assuming those days are over."

"Over and done with."

"That's good to know."

"You have my word. I don't want anyone but you."

I tried to think of the best way to approach the issue of bad sex. I'd once read that you should never come right out and tell a man that he's lousy in bed. Not if you still want to deal with him. Negative statements about a man's sex skills have been known to cause impotency. I chose the subtle approach.

"Trevor, I've been thinking. Maybe we could get a little freakier in the bedroom."

"Baby, I can get as freaky as you want me to get. You know what I'm working with."

"Yes, I do." Not much, I thought. "Trevor, let's go upstairs."

"Sure."

I led him up the steps to the master bedroom.

"Now that you have me up here, what do you plan to do with me?" he asked.

"I plan to play a little game with you."

"What type of game?"

"Lie down on your back."

Trevor grinned and lay on the bed. "Mary Ann, you have no idea how much I've missed you. Even before you left town, it seemed like you were ignoring me."

I decided to be honest. "I was avoiding you, Trevor."

He raised his brows. "Why?"

"Because I had a lot to think about," I replied, licking my lips. "Things happened rather quickly between us and I wasn't sure I was ready to take the next step."

Trevor propped himself up on his elbows. "I realize that my reputation preceded me. Patricia, in particular, filled your head with a bunch of nonsense and lies."

"What Patricia told me wasn't nonsense and lies to her. The women you've been dealing with are real people with real emotions. I think men forget that sometimes."

He winced. "I can admit to that. But you have to understand

that I was raised a certain way. I come from a household where my dad openly cheated on my mother and talked to her any kind of way."

"So that makes it okay to treat other women like that?"

"No, that's not what I'm saying."

"I hope not because I am definitely not the one. I come from a loving background and I have never once seen my father disrespect my mother. I expect and will accept nothing less than the same. Let's get that straight from the start."

"I feel you," he said.

"Do you really?"

He nodded.

"I sincerely hope so because no matter how well you think you know me, there is much more to me. That shit with FeFe or anything like it better not ever happen again. If you cheat on me, I better not find out about it."

"Mary Ann, I'll never cheat on you again. I know that you'll never cheat on me so I plan to show you the same consideration."

I smirked. If he only knew how much cheating I would be doing. Like Aunt Venus said, though, what he doesn't know . . .

I went over to Trevor's dresser and took out the blindfold he used to sleep in late. He was sensitive to light. I climbed on top of him on the bed and blindfolded him.

"Aw, so this is your game!"

"This is only the beginning of my game." I stood up, kicked off my boots, and pulled down my tights and underwear. "Trevor, no matter what I do to you, promise you won't touch me with your hands."

"What?"

"I'm not going to tie you up. We're going to work on the honor system. But if you touch me, game's over, I'm getting dressed, going back—"

"You're naked?" he asked excitedly.

"Don't worry about that!" I lashed out at him. "I'm in charge so shut the fuck up!"

Trevor laughed. "Hmm, I get it. You're playing that dominatrix shit out. I can get with that. I think it's kinky. I'll be your sex slave."

I rolled my eyes. "Like I said, if you touch me, the game's over, I'm getting dressed, going back to my dorm, and never speaking to you again. No more relationship, no moving in together, nothing."

He frowned. "Are you serious?"

"Very serious. Try me and see what happens."

"But what if I get so aroused that I can't control myself?"

"That's the whole point of the game: learning self-control. You're too used to having your way. You need to learn a lesson."

Trevor sighed. "I'll try it, Mary Ann, but I can't guarantee—"

"Listen, *slave,* I'm not fucking around with you. You say you want to be with me."

"I do."

"Then prove it. Do everything I say and do nothing I don't say. It's simple. Those are the only rules. Now repeat the rules."

"Do everything you say and do nothing you don't say."

I pushed him back on the bed. "Again."

"Do everything you say and do nothing you don't say."

"Very good, *slave*." I finished taking off my clothes. "Now, the first thing I want you to do is sit up with your back against the headboard."

After he'd done as I instructed, I stood on the bed with my feet straddling his hips. I lifted my left leg and placed it over Trevor's shoulder. "Eat me. Eat me good."

Trevor started doing his normal lousy pussy-eating.

"Stop!" I yelled at him. "My clit is not a doughnut. You're not supposed to take bites out of it. Now try it again. This time, lick it in long, slow strokes."

There was an immediate improvement. Trevor pushed his hands down between the mattress and headboard so he wouldn't be tempted to touch me. It was comical but I held back the laugh since I was being dominant.

"Um, that's better," I said. "Now stick the tip of your tongue deep into my pussy and wriggle it around. What does it taste like?"

Trevor took his tongue out for a second and whispered, "Like candy."

"That's right. It is candy and you better cherish it every minute of every day. Now eat."

I spent the rest of the night "training" Trevor. He showed a lot of potential I never knew existed. That just goes to show that men are not psychic and therefore women have to learn to speak up. Men never hesitate about what they want sexually. If they want you to suck their dick, they tell you. If they want you to lick their balls, they tell you. If they want you to bend over so they can hit it from the back, they tell you. But women tend to shy away from expressing their wants and desires.

The next morning I lay in bed counting my blessings. I was grateful that Patricia and Olive had entered my life. Otherwise, I would have been sexually repressed forever. Even if I had still ended up with Trevor, I would have been content to just satisfy him. Life's way too short for that. I was grateful for my aunt Venus for making me realize it was okay to become a member of Alpha Phi Fuckem.

An inkling of guilt still existed. I had the feeling that Trevor was done with his playa ways and I was just beginning. I was ready to make the lifetime commitment to APF; no matter what

28

olive

The time for Mary Ann's induction had arrived and I was probably more excited than she was. The ceremonies always did something to me; it was like a rebirth every time. This ceremony was going to be a particularly special one since Venus was Mary Ann's aunt. Not only did she fly into town for the occasion but all of the remaining founders came.

We held the ritual in the mansion of the senator. Talk about a woman with style and grace. Her constituents would have dropped dead on the spot if they found out, and tabloids would have had a field day. But the senator was confident she had nothing to worry about, and she didn't.

We began at midnight. The semblance of a new day. The

semblance of a new life. Mary Ann was led into the center of the ballroom where the founders were dressed in gold robes and the other members were dressed in red robes. We all stood in a large circle.

Mary Ann wore the traditional gold APF teddy and was chained together by two locks. She was also blindfolded.

"Mary Ann Ferguson," Venus began, "you have been selected to become one of the illustrious sorors of Alpha Phi Fuckem Sorority. This is an honor that you shall not take lightly. Many have come but few are chosen. This is not a temporary position. This is a lifetime position. You must exhibit the poise, style, and grace of Alpha Phi Fuckem at all times."

The senator took over from there. "As a member of Alpha Phi Fuckem Sorority, you must understand these things. You must *never* reveal our organization to anyone unless they are a candidate for membership and only after discussing it with the other members of your chapter. You must *never* stop pursuing your professional goals and it is your responsibility to guide and encourage others in attaining theirs. Particularly, women of color. You must become a mentor in your community. You must be the best you can be at anything you choose to do. You must *never* forget that as a woman, you are entitled to sexual satisfaction. Do not allow anyone to make you think otherwise, and do not allow anyone to treat you in a manner undeserving."

Another founding member, a judge from Detroit, went next. "Alpha Phi Fuckem must go to your grave with you. Tonight, you will be given a handbook. No one else must ever see it. *Not ever!* Now, let the official induction begin."

As the two members that had "discovered" Mary Ann, Patricia and I were entrusted to do the "freedom from bondage" ceremony. I approached Mary Ann and stood on her right side while Patricia stood on her left.

Patricia said, "Mary Ann, you are chained together by two locks. One represents the bondage of your body and the other represents the bondage of your mind." She removed a key from the pocket of her robe and started undoing the lock on her side. "I am freeing your body. From now on it belongs only to you. It is your temple and you must treat it as such. Only give it to those you wish. Always practice safe sex. Stay healthy. Live long."

Patricia let the lock drop to the floor. I removed a key from the pocket of my robe and undid the other lock. "I am freeing your mind. From now on, leave it open. Never imagine that something is beneath you, above or beyond you. Our bodies were freed from slavery a long time ago. If we can free our bodies, then we can also free our minds. Consider yours free."

Patricia and I finished removing the chains and rejoined the circle of sorors.

Venus came forward with the official Alpha Phi Fuckem scepter. She touched Mary Ann's left shoulder with it and then her right. "Mary Ann Ferguson, from this moment on, you will be known by another name. From this moment on, you are officially a soror. From this moment on, you will be the one known as Soror Ride Dick." Venus turned to the others. "So be it?"

We all said in unison, "So be it!"

Venus removed the blindfold from Mary Ann's eyes and hugged her. "Congratulations, soror!"

"Thanks, Aunt Venus!" Mary Ann exclaimed.

Venus touched her lips. "No, not Aunt Venus. Soror Fornication."

They grinned at each other and hugged again.

The rest of the evening went beautifully. Mary Ann was presented with the Alpha Phi Fuckem Handbook, charm necklace, jacket, paddle, and other items including the custom-made Alpha Phi Fuckem dildo and vibrator.

We ate and drank until sunrise before we went our separate ways until next time. Who would be the next?

www.alphaphifuckem.com
You didn't know?